DARING THE DRAKARN WARRIOR LORD

A DRAKARN HOLIDAY NOVELLA

DRAKARN MATES

KATE RUDOLPH

Deck the halls with blades and fury...

Terra has claimed her place beside Darrokar, her fierce Drakarn mate, but not everyone sees her as worthy. When her honor is challenged, she refuses to back down. The only way to prove herself is to enter the deadly Skalanth trials... even when her mate forbids it.

The trials are designed to break the weak.

But Terra is no fragile thing. When she faces Darrokar in the final test, love and fury ignite... and the forge will decide if they burn apart or rise together.

We wish you a fiery Skalanth, and a forge-lit new year...

TERRA

THE CLANG of training blades rang in my ears.

My muscles burned. Sweat dripped down my spine, soaking through the thin shirt I wore. But I didn't stop moving. Couldn't stop. Not when Darrokar circled me like this, wings half-spread, golden eyes tracking every shift of my weight.

I lunged.

He parried, the screech of metal on metal singing through the cavern. The impact jarred up my arms, but I used the momentum, spinning away before his tail could sweep my legs. The heat crystals overhead cast everything in shades of fire and shadow, turning the smooth patches of floor into mirrors of light.

"Better," he said, voice rough. "But predictable."

I bared my teeth. "Then stop me."

He moved.

God, he was fast for someone his size. Seven feet of scaled muscle and lethal grace, closing the distance before I could blink. I brought my blade up, angling it to redirect rather than meet his strength head-on. The training sword was blunted, but still heavy as hell and it slid along his with a shriek that made my ears ring.

Then his free hand caught my wrist.

I twisted, using a joint lock I'd drilled a thousand times, but his grip was iron. Scaled, heated iron that sent sparks racing up my arm. Not pain. Something else entirely. Something that made my breath hitch even as I drove my knee toward his midsection.

He blocked with his thigh, and suddenly we were grappling, blades forgotten as we fought for position. His chest pressed against mine, and I could feel every breath he took, every rumble building in his throat. The scent of him, smoke and stone and *mine* flooded my senses.

I hooked my foot behind his ankle and shoved.

It almost worked.

Almost.

But then his wings flared, balance perfect, and he turned the momentum against me. The world spun. My back hit the floor, firm enough to knock the air from my lungs. His weight followed, pinning me, one hand catching both my wrists and pressing them above my head.

"Yield," he growled.

I bucked against him, testing his hold. Solid. Unmoving. Heat radiated from every point of contact, seeping through my clothes, into my skin. My heart hammered against my ribs, and I couldn't tell if it was from exertion or the way he was looking at me.

Like he wanted to devour me.

"Make me," I said.

His eyes flashed. The hand not restraining my wrists slid down my side, claws catching on fabric. Not tearing. Not yet. Just a promise of what those talons could do.

"Careful what you demand, *luvae.*"

The endearment wove around me tight. Low and possessive, wrapped in that gravelly tone that made my stomach clench. I should have been thinking tactically, looking for an escape, a reversal. Instead, all I could focus on was the press of his hips against mine, the way his scales felt against my overheated skin.

"I'm not afraid of you," I said, and it was true. I'd never been afraid of him. Not even in the beginning.

"I know." His head dipped, breath hot against my throat. "That's the problem."

Then his mouth was on my neck, fangs grazing the sensitive skin there. Not biting. Just pressure, just the threat of it, and a sound escaped me that was definitely not tactical.

Screw it.

I arched into him, and his grip on my wrists tightened. The rumble in his chest deepened, vibrating through me. His tongue, long and clever and absolutely sinful, traced the line of my pulse, and I felt the exact moment his control started to fray.

"Terra." My name sounded wrecked. "We're supposed to—"

"Shut up and kiss me."

He did.

His mouth claimed mine with a hunger that stole what little breath I'd regained. No gentleness, no hesitation. Just raw need and the taste of him flooding my senses. I kissed him back just as fiercely, biting his lower lip, feeling the sharp points of his fangs against my tongue.

His hand released my wrists, but I didn't pull away. Instead, I buried my fingers in the thick hair at the base of his skull, holding him to me. His claws found the hem of my shirt, and this time he did tear, the sound of rending fabric loud in the quiet chamber.

Cool air hit my skin for a heartbeat before his palm covered my breast, scaled and hot and perfect. I gasped into his mouth, and he swallowed the sound, his kiss turning deeper, more demanding.

I got my hands on his chest, feeling the hard planes of muscle beneath his own training shirt. I needed to feel his skin. His scales. The contrast of textures that never failed to undo me.

He broke the kiss long enough to yank his shirt over his head, wings shifting to accommodate the movement. The sight of him, bare-chested, eyes molten, lips swollen from my kisses, sent a fresh surge of want through me.

"You're wearing too many clothes," he said, voice like gravel.

"Fix it."

He did, with an efficiency that would have

been impressive if I wasn't so focused on getting my hands back on him. My shirt joined his somewhere to the left. My pants followed, his claws making quick work of laces and fabric until I was bare beneath him.

The stone floor should have been cold. It wasn't. Heat radiated up from it, the same geothermal warmth that kept all of Scalvaris livable. Or maybe it was just us, burning hot enough to warm the rock itself.

Darrokar's gaze raked over me, and I felt it like a touch. Possessive. Hungry. Reverent.

"Mine," he said, and it wasn't a question.

"Yours," I agreed, reaching for the laces of his pants. "Now get these off before I rip them."

His laugh was dark, pleased. He stood just long enough to strip, and then he was covering me again, skin to scales, heat to heat. The weight of him should have been crushing. Instead, it felt right. Like this was exactly where I was meant to be.

His hand slid between my thighs, and I stopped thinking entirely.

The pads of his clever fingers, careful because of the claws, found exactly where I needed him. I bit back a moan, but he felt the tension in my body, the way I trembled under his touch.

"Don't hide from me," he murmured against my ear. "I want every sound."

Then he did something with his fingers that made me cry out, back arching off the floor. He made an approving noise, deep and rumbling, and did it again. And again. Building a rhythm that had me writhing, chasing the pleasure he offered.

"Darrokar." His name fell from my lips like a prayer. A curse. A demand.

"I have you, *luvae*." His thumb found the bundle of nerves that made stars burst behind my eyelids. "Let go."

I shattered.

The orgasm crashed through me, stealing my breath, my vision, everything but the sensation of his hands on me and his voice in my ear, murmuring words in his own language that I didn't need to understand to feel.

Before I could fully come down, he was moving, positioning himself between my thighs. The blunt head of his cock, already slick with that fluid his body produced, pressed against my entrance. I looked up at him, meeting those golden eyes, and saw my own need reflected back.

He pushed in, slow and careful, giving me time to adjust. The stretch was intense, pleasure-pain that made me gasp. The scales at the base of his cock rasped against my sensitive flesh, and the ridges along his length dragged in all the right ways.

But it was the tip, that independently moving piece of flesh that seemed designed specifically to drive me insane, that made me moan. It flexed inside me, seeking, stroking, finding spots I hadn't known existed.

"God," I breathed.

"Just me," he corrected, voice strained. Then he was moving, pulling out and thrusting back in, setting a pace that had me clinging to his shoulders.

The training chamber filled with the sounds of us, skin on scales, harsh breathing, the wet slide of our bodies joining. His tail wrapped around my thigh, holding me open for him, and I couldn't have closed my legs if I'd wanted to.

I didn't want to.

I wanted it, the overwhelming fullness, the drag of his cock against my inner walls, the way that flexible tip curled and stroked with each thrust. I wanted the weight of him above me, the heat of his breath on my skin, the possessive grip of his hands on my hips.

"Harder," I demanded, nails digging into his shoulders.

He complied with a snarl, hips snapping forward with enough force to make me see stars. The angle shifted, and suddenly, that clever tip was pressing against a spot that made my entire body lock up.

"There," I gasped. "Right there, don't stop—"

He didn't. He drove into me with single-minded focus, hitting that spot with every thrust, and I felt the pressure building again. Faster this time. Sharper.

His fangs found my shoulder, not breaking skin but applying pressure, and that was it. I came with a cry that echoed off the stone walls, clenching around him, body shaking with the force of it.

He followed with a roar, hips jerking as he spilled inside me. I felt every pulse, every wave, the heat of him filling me as that flexible tip continued to stroke, drawing out both our pleasure until we were both trembling.

He collapsed beside me, careful not to crush me, wings spread across the floor. For a long moment, we just lay there, chests heaving, skin cooling in the chamber's heat.

Then he reached out, pulling me against his side. I went willingly, tucking myself against him, one leg thrown over his hip. His tail curled around my calf, a casual possessiveness that made me smile.

"I should let you win more often," I said when I could speak again.

His laugh rumbled through his chest. "You didn't let me do anything, *luvae*. I earned that victory."

"Keep telling yourself that."

He nipped my ear in retaliation, and I grinned. This, the teasing, the ease between us, was almost as good as the sex.

Eventually, we had to move. The stone floor wasn't exactly comfortable for extended lounging. Darrokar stood first, offering me a hand. I took it, letting him pull me to my feet, and tried not to wince at the pleasant ache between my thighs.

We gathered our scattered clothes. Most of mine were beyond saving, shredded by enthusiastic claws. Darrokar looked entirely too pleased about that.

"I'm running out of training clothes," I pointed out.

"I'll have more made."

"And then you'll just destroy those too."

"Yes." No shame whatsoever in that admission.

I shook my head, pulling on his shirt instead. It fell to mid-thigh on me, and his eyes darkened seeing me in it.

"Don't even think about it," I warned. "I can barely walk as it is."

"Later, then."

"Insatiable lizard."

"Your insatiable lizard."

I couldn't argue with that.

We made our way back to his quarters—our quarters, I corrected myself. After eight months in Scalvaris, the place was almost starting to feel like home. The rooms were quiet, lit by the ever-present heat crystals. Darrokar headed for the bathing pool, but I caught his hand.

"Wait. I have something for you."

He turned, curiosity crossing his features. "Something?"

I crossed to where I'd hidden my surprise earlier, tucked behind one of the obsidian pillows on the lounge. The package was small, wrapped in cloth I'd traded for from one of the Scalvaris artisans.

"Here," I said, offering it to him.

He took it carefully, claws gentle on the fabric. "What is this?"

I rolled my eyes. "Open it and find out."

He did, unwrapping the cloth with a precision that made me smile. I'd worked with Vyne in secret for weeks, describing what I wanted, helping to forge it myself.

It was a ring designed to fit over his knuckle, crafted from a piece of metal I'd salvaged from our crashed ship. I'd spent hours shaping it, polishing it until it gleamed like silver.

"*Luvae*," he breathed, holding the ring up to the light. "You made this yourself?"

I nodded, suddenly shy. "I helped. I know it's not much, but, well, it's Christmas. Ish."

He slipped the ring over the knuckles of his right hand, flexing his fingers to test the fit. It looked perfect there, like it belonged. "You mark me as yours, *luvae*," he said, his voice rough with emotion.

Before I could respond, he reached for me, pulling me across his lap until I was straddling his thighs. His hands framed my face, thumbs stroking across my cheekbones as he studied my features like he was memorizing them.

"It is exquisite work. But what is Christmas?"

He had trouble fitting the syllables around his tongue. "It's an Earth thing. A tradition." I settled onto him. "Back home, we celebrate it during winter. We give gifts, share meals, relax for just a bit."

He seemed confused. "We have no such tradition here."

"I know. That's why I'm not upset that you didn't get me a gift." I had to laugh at his sudden, slightly panicked expression.

He looked at the ring for a long time before slipping it onto his index finger. "You honor me."

He kissed me then, soft and sweet, so different from the desperate claiming in the training chamber. It was tender. Reverent.

Right.

When he pulled back, there was a smile on his face. "The other warriors will think I've gone soft."

"Let them think what they want."

"Rath will never let me hear the end of it."

I grinned. "Rath can mind his own business." And I happened to know for a fact that Rath would be getting a Christmas gift of his own from his mate.

Darrokar laughed, the sound warm and genuine. Then he sobered slightly, and I saw the shift in his expression—from mate to Warrior Lord.

"The Skalanth begins in three days."

I groaned. Darrokar had been boring me with news of the ritual preparations for weeks. Apparently, the Skalanth was a big deal. The annual warrior trial where every trainee and young warrior tried to prove themselves. It was part competition, part rite of passage, and entirely dangerous.

"You haven't been able to hide your enthusiasm for it," I observed sarcastically.

"The Skalanth is necessary. It tests skill, builds unity, honors tradition." He sounded like he was reciting from a manual. Then his shoulders slumped slightly. "But every year, some young fool tries to attempt a challenge far beyond their capability. For glory. For recognition."

"And you have to keep them from killing themselves."

"Exactly." He scrubbed a hand over his face. "Last year, a trainee barely out of his juvenile training tried to fight Khorlar. Khorlar, who has forgotten more about combat than this whelp had ever learned."

"What happened?"

"Khorlar knocked him unconscious in under a minute. Gently, by his standards. The trainee woke with nothing but bruised pride and a valuable lesson."

I could picture it perfectly. Khorlar's stone-faced expression as he efficiently dismantled an overconfident youngster. "At least he learned."

"Some do. Others require multiple lessons." Darrokar's tail lashed in irritation. "And the senior warriors must balance allowing them to test themselves with preventing actual harm."

"Sounds exhausting."

"I'll be busy managing egos, preventing disasters, and trying to identify which trainees actually have potential versus which ones simply have bravado."

I leaned against his shoulder, offering silent support. This was part of his role, not just leading in battle, but shepherding the next generation. Making sure Scalvaris had warriors worthy of the name.

"You'll manage," I said. "You always do."

"With significantly more gray scales each year."

"You don't have any gray scales."

"Give it time. This Skalanth will likely produce several."

I laughed, pressing a kiss to his jaw. "Poor suffering Warrior Lord. However will you cope?"

He pulled me into his lap, arms banding around my waist. "Careful, *luvae*. I can think of several ways you could help me cope."

He kissed me, and I moaned into it.

A mate's work was never done.

2

DARROKAR

THE RING CAUGHT the light as I flexed my fingers.

Terra's gift gleamed against my dark scales, the metal bright where it wrapped around my knuckle. I'd worn it since the moment she'd given it to me, and each time I caught sight of it, something warm unfurled in my chest.

She'd marked me as surely as I'd claimed her, and I wore her declaration with more pride than any battle scar.

The corridors leading to the Forge Temple stretched before me, carved from the mountain's heart. Heat crystals embedded in the walls pulsed with dull red light. The air grew thicker here, heavy with incense and the weight of centuries. Every surface bore the marks of devotion: sigils etched into stone, offerings left in alcoves, the bones of the mountain itself shaped into reverence.

I'd never loved this place.

The Temple served its purpose. The priests maintained traditions, blessed warriors before battle, oversaw the sacred rites that bound our society together. But there was something oppressive about these halls, something that made my wings want to spread even though the space wouldn't allow it.

Maybe it was the way sound died here, swallowed by stone and ceremony. Maybe it was knowing that Karyseth walked these passages, her fanaticism seeping into the very rock.

Still, I came. The Skalanth required the Temple's participation, and I wouldn't give Karyseth the satisfaction of thinking I feared her domain.

The preparations should be well underway by now. The blood-flame needed to be readied, the ceremonial chambers prepared, the blessing rites scheduled. Jalliun had assured me everything would be handled, but I preferred to see for myself.

I rounded a corner and stopped.

Voices carried from ahead, raised in a way that violated every protocol of temple grounds. Arguing. Here, where even footsteps were supposed to be measured and soft.

I recognized both speakers immediately.

"You twist the teachings to suit your own agenda." Karyseth's voice could have frozen lava. "The ancestors never intended for our sacred spaces to be contaminated by outsider influence."

"The ancestors valued strength and adaptation." Jalliun's response came quieter but no less firm. "They built Scalvaris to endure, not to stagnate. Refusing to evolve is not preservation, it's suicide."

"Careful, priest. Your words border on heresy."

"Truth often does, in the ears of those who fear it."

The passage opened into a small antechamber, one of dozens that branched off the main temple corridors. Karyseth stood with her back to a carved altar, her scales catching the light. Jalliun faced her, shoulders squared, his deep green coloring almost black in the shadows.

"The humans are here." Jalliun's hands remained steady at his sides. "Mated to our finest warriors. They've proven their worth in combat, in strategy, in healing. Denying their value doesn't erase their presence."

"Their presence *is* the problem." Karyseth's wings rustled. "Every day they remain, they corrupt. They weaken. They teach our warriors to value softness over strength, sentiment over duty."

"They teach our warriors that strength comes in many forms."

"They teach our warriors to forget what they are."

The venom in her words made my fangs ache. I'd heard this before, in Council chambers and whispered conversations, but hearing it here, in the Temple's heart, felt different. More dangerous. Karyseth didn't just disapprove of Terra and her brethren. She hated them with the kind of cold certainty that led to violence.

"What I am," Jalliun said, "is a priest who serves Scalvaris. All of Scalvaris. Not just the parts that conform to your vision of purity."

Karyseth's laugh was sharp enough to draw blood. "Your vision will destroy us."

I chose that moment to step into the light.

Both priests turned, and I watched the argument drain from their postures. Jalliun's expression shifted to respectful acknowledgment. Karyseth's face could have been carved from the same stone as the altar behind her.

"Warrior Lord." She inclined her head, the gesture technically correct but empty of any real deference. "We did not expect you so early."

"Clearly." I let my gaze move between them, making it obvious I'd heard enough. "I trust the preparations are proceeding smoothly, despite the … theological debate."

Jalliun had the grace to look somewhat abashed. Karyseth simply stared at me, and I felt the exact moment her attention fixed on my hand.

On the ring.

Her eyes narrowed. Something flickered across her face, too quick to name but cold enough to feel. When she spoke again, her voice could have stripped flesh from bone.

"I see you wear your corruption proudly, Warrior Lord."

My claws flexed. The ring caught the light again, deliberate. "I wear a gift from my mate. As is my right."

"A gift of foreign influence worming its way into the highest levels of our leadership." She took a step forward, and the temperature in the room seemed to drop despite the heat crystals. "How long before foreign ideas follow? Foreign loyalties? How long before Scalvaris becomes something unrecognizable, led by a Warrior Lord who values his human's trinkets over his people's traditions?"

The accusation hung in the air.

I could have roared. Could have reminded her exactly who led Scalvaris, who commanded the Blade Council, who'd earned his position through blood and victory and years of service. Could have put her in her place with the kind of authority that left no room for question.

Instead, I smiled.

"My mate," I said, voice soft, "crafted this ring with her own hands. Worked the forge alongside Vyne, learned our techniques, honored our methods. She took metal from her fallen ship, the last piece of her old world, and shaped it into something new. Something that bridges what was with what is." I held up my hand, letting the ring gleam. "If you see corruption in that, High Priestess, perhaps the problem lies not with the gift, but with the eyes that view it."

Karyseth's scales rippled—a tell she couldn't quite control. Fury. But she was too calculated to let it loose, not here, not now. Instead, she drew herself up, wings folding tight against her back.

"The Skalanth will proceed as tradition demands," she said. "The Temple will fulfill its duties, as we always have. I trust the Warrior Lord will do the same."

It wasn't quite a dismissal. She didn't have the authority for that. But it was close enough to make the insult clear.

She turned and swept from the antechamber, her tail leaving a trail in the dust. I watched her go, tracking the rigid line of her spine, the controlled fury in every movement. She'd retreat now, regroup, plan. Karyseth never acted on impulse. That's what made her dangerous.

When her footsteps finally faded, Jalliun released a breath.

"My apologies, Warrior Lord. That was … unseemly."

I waved off his concern. "Karyseth's opinions

are no secret. Better to hear them directly than whispered behind closed doors."

"Still. The Temple should present a unified front, especially during the Skalanth." He moved to one of the wall alcoves, adjusting an offering that had been knocked askew during the argument. "The discord serves no one."

"Discord has always existed. We just pretend otherwise during ceremonies."

That earned me a slight smile. "A cynical view for a Warrior Lord."

"Sit through a council meeting and tell me otherwise."

Jalliun's smile widened fractionally. He was younger than Karyseth by at least two decades, his scales still vibrant green without the fading that came with age. But his eyes held the kind of weariness that had nothing to do with years.

Fighting battles within your own institution did that.

"The preparations are nearly complete," he said, shifting to safer ground. "The ceremonial chamber has been cleansed and blessed. The offering stones have been placed. All that remains is the blood-flame itself."

"And that's ready?"

"Nyx has been overseeing the final stages. You know how particular he is about the work." Jalliun gestured deeper into the temple. "He should be in the preparation chamber now, if you wish to inspect it yourself."

I did. Not because I doubted Nyx's competence, but because seeing the blood-flame, holding it, feeling its heat, made the Skalanth real in a way that reports and schedules couldn't match.

"Thank you, Jalliun." I started toward the passage he'd indicated, then paused. "Your position can't be easy."

He met my gaze steadily. "My position is to serve the Temple and the city. Sometimes those duties align. Sometimes they don't. I do what I believe is right."

I left him there, his silhouette dark against the crystal's light, and headed deeper into the Temple's warren.

The preparation chamber sat at the end of a corridor that sloped downward, taking me closer to the mountain's molten heart. The heat intensified with every step, pressing against my scales. Most Drakarn found it uncomfortable. I'd always liked it. Heat meant the forge, and the forge meant creation. Weapons born from fire and will.

I stepped through and found Nyx bent over the sacred forge, his steel-gray scales slicked with sweat and soot. He didn't look up, focused entirely on the piece before him. The blood-flame rested in a cradle of heat-resistant stone, glowing with an inner light born of forge fire.

Beautiful.

The gem was the size of my fist, multifaceted, each surface catching and throwing light in shades of red and gold. It pulsed like a heartbeat, warm and alive. Legend said it had been cut from the mountain's core when Scalvaris was first founded, blessed by the original priests, bathed in the blood of the first Warrior Lord. The blood-flame was sacred, and retrieving it from the Temple's heart was the goal of the Skalanth.

Nyx turned. Soot streaked his face, and his wings hung loose with exhaustion, but satisfaction gleamed in his eyes.

"Warrior Lord." He inclined his head, then grinned. "Come to check my work?"

"Come to make sure you haven't burned down the Temple."

"The day's still young."

I moved closer to the forge, feeling the heat wash over me. The blood-flame's glow intensified as I approached, responding to presence the way it always did. Some said it recognized warriors. Others claimed it simply reacted to intent. I'd never cared about the why, only the what.

"It's perfect," I said.

"Of course it is. I'm not some novice." Nyx wiped his hands on a cloth, leaving gray smears. Then his gaze caught on my hand, and his grin widened. "That's new."

I held up the ring, letting him see it properly. "A gift."

"From your human." Not a question. Nyx had always been perceptive. "Fine work. Vyne's?"

"Terra's hands, Vyne's guidance."

Nyx whistled low. "She worked the forge herself?"

"She did."

"And Karyseth probably lost her mind seeing it."

I laughed, the sound echoing off stone walls. "She did."

Nyx circled the forge, checking seals and temperature levels. "The blood-flame is ready for placement. I'll have it moved to the inner sanctum before dawn. Then we wait for the novices to try their damnedest."

"How many do you think will attempt it?"

"Attempt? Dozens. Actually reach it?" He shrugged, wings rustling. "Maybe three. Maybe none. The inner sanctum's defenses are particularly creative this year. And they'll have to get by us."

I raised an eyebrow. "Creative how?"

"You'll see. I'm not spoiling the surprise."

"Nyx."

"Warrior Lord." He matched my tone perfectly, mockingly formal. "Some things are better experienced than explained. Trust me, the trainees will have quite the challenge."

I did trust him. Nyx had been designing trial courses for longer than some of the trainees had been alive. If he said it was challenging, bones would probably be broken. Non-fatally. I hoped.

Nyx knew as well as I did that war was coming. We needed to test our warriors, not end them.

I moved around the forge, examining the setup. Everything was precisely arranged, tools hung in order, the blood-flame's cradle positioned for optimal heat exposure. Nyx's work always had that quality, meticulous and uncompromising. It's what made him such an effective Shield, both in title and practice.

"Race you," I said.

Nyx's head snapped up. "What?"

I nodded toward the blood-flame. "First one to the inner sanctum and past all your traps wins."

"That's sacrilege."

"That's a challenge." I grinned, feeling something loosen in my chest. When was the last time I'd done something purely for the joy of it? Not duty, not politics, not carefully calculated leadership. Just two warriors testing each other because they could. "Unless you're worried I'll win."

That did it.

Nyx's eyes flashed. "You're on."

We moved simultaneously.

I launched myself toward the passage leading deeper into the Temple, wings snapping open to catch air in the high-ceilinged chamber. Nyx went low, using his smaller frame to dart through the forge equipment, taking a route I couldn't follow.

The inner sanctum lay three levels down, through corridors that twisted and doubled back on themselves. I knew the path. So did Nyx. The question was who could navigate it faster.

I tucked my wings and dove into a narrow

passage, claws finding purchase on walls as I half-ran, half-flew through the space. Behind me, I heard Nyx's talons clicking against stone, gaining ground. The corridor opened into a vertical shaft, and I spread my wings fully, spiraling downward in a controlled fall.

Nyx dropped past me, wings folded completely, trusting gravity and his own reflexes. He snapped his wings open at the last possible moment, pulling up with precision that would've been impressive if it wasn't so damn annoying.

He hit the next level first.

I followed, landing hard enough to crack the stone beneath my feet. Nyx was already moving, and I chased him through a series of chambers that blurred together. Heat crystals flashed past. Carved pillars became obstacles to dodge. The Temple's sacred quiet shattered under the sound of our passage.

Nyx took a sharp turn into a side corridor, and I realized his strategy. He was using the defensive measures meant for the trainees, the traps and barriers that would slow anyone who didn't know the sanctum's secrets.

I took a different route, one that required squeezing through a gap barely wide enough for my shoulders. My scales scraped against stone, and I felt something tear, but I was through. The shortcut put me ahead, and I poured on speed.

The inner sanctum's entrance appeared before me, a circular door carved with protective sigils. I hit it with my shoulder, and it swung inward, revealing the chamber beyond.

The empty pedestal where the blood-flame would soon rest stood in the center of the room. I crossed the distance in three strides, reaching for it, ready to touch and claim my victory.

Nyx slammed into me from the side.

We went down in a tangle of wings and limbs, rolling across the sanctum floor. I got an elbow into his ribs. He raked claws across my shoulder, not deep enough to seriously injure but enough to sting. We grappled, testing strength against strength, and I remembered why Nyx had earned his title.

The bastard was immovable when he wanted to be.

I hooked my tail around his ankle and yanked. He went down, but took me with him, and we crashed into the pedestal.

I was faster.

"I win."

Nyx lay on his back, chest heaving, and started to laugh. Deep, genuine laughter that filled the sanctum and probably violated a dozen different temple protocols. I couldn't help it. I laughed too, the sound mixing with his until we were both shaking with it.

"You cheated," Nyx managed between gasps.

"I was creative."

"You nearly broke the pedestal."

I gave it a gentle shove. It didn't move. "It's sturdy. It's fine."

Nyx sat up, wings dragging on the floor, and shook his head. Soot and dust covered both of us, and I was pretty sure I was bleeding from at least two places. Worth it. Entirely worth it for this moment of pure, uncomplicated joy.

"Warrior Lord Darrokar, what exactly do you think you're doing?"

We both froze.

Jalliun stood in the sanctum entrance, arms crossed, expression caught somewhere between exasperation and amusement. He looked at us, at the disturbed pedestal, and sighed.

"Desecrating sacred space," he said. "Disturbing holy relics. Brawling in the inner sanctum. Shall I continue?"

I carefully placed the blood-flame back on its pedestal. "We were … testing the defenses."

"Testing." Jalliun's tone suggested he didn't believe that for a moment.

"Thoroughly," Nyx added, climbing to his feet. "Very thorough testing."

"I see." Jalliun stepped into the sanctum, and I caught the twitch at the corner of his mouth. He was trying not to smile. "And your professional assessment of these defenses?"

"Adequate," I said.

"Could use some work," Nyx said at the same time.

Jalliun did smile then, brief but genuine. "I'm sure the trainees will appreciate your dedication to their safety." He moved to the pedestal, checking for cracks. "Fortunately, no actual harm done. Though I shudder to think what Karyseth would say if she'd witnessed this."

"She'd probably declare us both corrupted beyond redemption," I said.

"She might not be wrong."

Maybe this year's Skalanth wouldn't be the burden I'd anticipated. Maybe, with the right perspective, it could be something more. A celebration of what we were and what we were becoming.

"The blood-flame will be ready," Jalliun said, his tone shifting back to business. "I'll have the sanctum cleansed and re-blessed before the trials begin. Try not to destroy anything else in the meantime."

"No promises," Nyx said cheerfully.

Jalliun shook his head and left, his footsteps fading into the temple's depths. Nyx and I followed at a more leisurely pace, our earlier race abandoned in favor of walking side by side through the corridors.

"Your human's changed you," Nyx said after a while. "In a good way."

We emerged into the main temple corridor, and I paused, looking back toward the inner sanctum. In a few days, trainees would attempt that same path we'd just raced. They'd struggle and fail and try again, pushing themselves toward something greater. Some would succeed. Most wouldn't. But all of them would learn.

That's what the Skalanth was supposed to be. A crucible, yes. But also a forge. A place where warriors were shaped and tempered and made stronger.

"This might actually be enjoyable," I said.

Nyx clapped me on the shoulder, careful of the scratches he'd left earlier. "That's the spirit. Now come on. If we're going to oversee this thing, we should probably look less like we've been rolling around in the forge."

"You started it."

"You challenged me."

"Details."

3

TERRA

EDEN WAS BALANCED on a chair that had seen better days, trying to tie a strip of salvaged parachute silk around a heat crystal. The fabric kept slipping through her fingers, and she was swearing under her breath, creative combinations that would've made my old drill sergeant proud.

"A little help here?" she called without looking back.

I crossed the space and steadied the chair. The human quarters weren't large, carved from the same volcanic stone as everything else in Scalvaris, but the women had done their best to make it feel less like a cave and more like home. Fabric panels hung on the walls, hiding the rough rock.

Cushions purchased in the market clustered in corners.

Right now, though, it looked like a craft project had exploded.

Polished stones covered every surface, arranged in patterns that probably meant something to whoever had placed them. Strips of metal and leather from the ceiling, catching light and throwing it back.

In the corner, Eden's pride and joy stood like a monument to optimism: a scraggly bush she'd gotten from *somewhere*, its branches covered in sharp needles and her determination to call it a tree.

"There." Eden tied off the silk and hopped down. "What do you think?"

"I think it looks like we robbed a salvage yard."

"It's the Space-Christmas aesthetic." She grinned, shoving hair out of her face. "We're pioneers. We're making new traditions."

"We're making a fire hazard," Rachel said from across the room. She stood near Eden's bush-tree, eyeing the candles arranged at its base with obvious concern. "One spark and the whole thing goes up."

Eden's grin only got bigger. "That's what makes it exciting."

"That's what makes it dangerous."

Eden stuck her tongue out. "Same thing."

I left them to argue and surveyed the rest of the space. Orla knelt by the makeshift kitchen, doing something complicated with spices and a pot that bubbled over the heat vent. Selene helped her, chopping something that looked vaguely root-like with a healer's precision. Hawk and Vega were attempting to hang more decorations, though it mostly involved Hawk making suggestions and Vega telling her why they wouldn't work.

Reika sat in the corner, small and quiet, watching everything with her too-wide eyes. Kinsley stayed close to her, not hovering but present, ready if needed. Kaiya had somehow gotten tangled in a length of silk and was trying to free herself without asking for help, too proud or too awkward to admit defeat.

My crew. My people. My responsibility.

It had been eight months since the crash. Eight months of survival, adaptation, and the slow, painful process of building something new from the wreckage of everything we'd lost. Some days it felt impossible. Others, like now, watching them laugh and argue and create joy out of scraps, it felt like maybe we'd actually make it.

"Terra, tell Rachel that space-Christmas needs candles," Eden demanded.

"Space-Christmas needs to not burn down our quarters," Rachel countered. "She's being a pyromaniac."

I held up my hands. "Compromise. Candles, but nowhere near the tree."

"It's a bush," Lexa called from where she was arranging stones into what might've been a menorah or might've been abstract art. "A sad, dying bush that Eden is torturing for aesthetic purposes."

"It's symbolic," Eden protested.

"It's botanical abuse," Vega jumped in on the fun.

Eden crossed her arms, her expression growing mulish. "You're all heathens with no appreciation for tradition."

"We have no idea if it's even close to December back home," Lexa pointed out, not for the first time. She'd been making this argument since Eden had proposed the celebration three weeks ago. "We could be celebrating in March for all we know."

"Does it matter?" Selene looked up from her chopping. "We're here. We're alive. And we need to live by this new calendar."

Something in her tone made the room go quiet. When Selene spoke, people listened. She had that quality, calm authority wrapped in gentleness, that made even her smallest observations feel profound.

The moment passed. Conversation resumed, overlapping and chaotic. I watched Kaiya finally extract herself from the silk, face flushed with embarrassment. Kinsley caught my eye and smiled, that warm, steady expression that said she had everything under control. Reika's fingers twisted in her lap, but she hadn't fled yet. She was getting braver by the day, and it didn't hurt that she had a freaking giant of a mate now to protect her when she needed it.

I moved to help Vega with the decorations. She handed me a length of wire, and we worked in easy silence.

Slowly, the quarters had transformed from cave to something almost festive, if you squinted and ignored the volcanic rock walls. The heat crystals cast everything in warm light. The makeshift ornaments reflected that glow. Eden's bush-tree stood in defiant celebration, needles and all.

"Okay," Eden announced, clapping her hands. "Candle time."

Rachel had won the argument about placement. The candles sat on a flat stone ledge away from anything flammable, arranged in a slightly wonky circle. If this was a metaphor, I wasn't really sure what for.

Earth was gone. Not destroyed, just unreachable. Somewhere across the impossible distance of space, life continued without us. People celebrated holidays we'd never see again. Seasons changed in patterns we'd never feel. Everything we'd known had become memory.

Eden lit the first candle.

"I miss my mom," she said quietly.

She passed the flame to Rachel, who lit the second candle with steady hands.

"My bubbe would tell me to buck up and make the most of this." Someone snorted, but I didn't catch who.

The flame moved around the circle. Each

woman lit a candle. Each woman named a loved one.

When the light reached Kira, she stared at it for a long moment. Her jaw worked. Her fingers trembled. But she lit her candle and spoke in a voice that cracked halfway through.

"For my sister. Wherever she is. I'm coming."

The flame came to me last. I looked at the eleven lit candles, at the faces of my people illuminated in their glow, and felt the weight of every choice that had brought us here.

"For the ones we couldn't save," I said. "And the ones we still can."

I lit the final candle.

We stood in silence, twelve flames burning against the dark. The makeshift decorations swayed in air currents. Somewhere in the distance, the sounds of Scalvaris continued, alien and familiar all at once.

Then Orla cleared her throat.

"Okay, enough sadness. Let's eat before this food gets cold."

"Thank freaking god," Lexa muttered.

We ate sitting on cushions on the floor, plates balanced on laps, passing dishes back and forth.

The conversation flowed easier now, loosened by food and the release of ceremony.

"So," Eden said around a mouthful of not-potato, "how are the mates?"

Hawk threw a piece of bread at her. "Subtle."

"I'm not here for subtle. I'm here for gossip." Eden grinned, unrepentant. "Come on. You're all mated to massive dragon warriors. There have to be stories."

"There are stories," Vega said dryly. "Most of them involve excessive protectiveness and an inability to understand the concept of personal space."

"Zarvash follows you around like a very large, scaly shadow," Selene observed.

"He does not."

"He absolutely does," Orla confirmed. "I've seen him lurking outside the training field when you're sparring."

Vega's face did something complicated. "He's not lurking. He's … strategically positioned."

"That's what lurking means," I said.

"You're one to talk." Vega pointed at me with her fork. "Darrokar nearly started a war last week because someone looked at you wrong."

"That someone was Karyseth, and she was threatening me."

"She was walking past you in a corridor."

"Aggressively." I shuddered.

Everyone laughed. Even Reika's mouth twitched.

"At least they're hot," Eden said wistfully. "That's something."

"You want a seven-foot dragon warrior?" Hawk asked. "I promise, they're not all they're cracked up to be."

I kept my mouth shut about *that*.

Eden sighed. "I've seen the way Khorlar looks at you. And I don't exactly see any human dudes around. And, no offense, but I don't think I'm going to fall for Lexa."

"Like I would have you." Lexa threw a piece of fruit at her.

Eden failed to dodge.

Next to her, Kira flinched.

She'd gone quiet again, pushing food around her plate without eating. Her shoulders hunched inward. Her gaze stayed fixed on nothing. I watched her fingers tighten on her fork, knuckles going white.

Lexa noticed too. She shifted closer, not obviously, just adjusting her position so she was within arm's reach. Ready.

Kira stood abruptly. "I can't." Her voice cracked. "I can't do this. I can't sit here celebrating while Larissa is—"

She didn't finish. Just turned and fled, the door to the quarters slamming behind her.

For a moment, nobody moved. Then Lexa was up and following, her own plate abandoned. The door closed again, softer this time.

The remaining ten of us sat in heavy silence.

"Damnit," Vega said.

"She's been holding that in for weeks," Selene said. "I knew it was coming."

"We all did," Kaiya said. Her plate sat untouched now too. "How long are we supposed to pretend this is okay? That we're safe while other humans are being tortured in Ignarath?"

"We're not pretending," I said.

"Aren't we?" Vega's eyes were hard. "We're decorating. Celebrating. Acting like we've built something stable here. But we haven't. We've just gotten comfortable while people suffer. You didn't see what they're doing out there." She shuddered.

"That's not fair," Orla said quietly.

"Isn't it?" Vega stood, her movement sharp.

"Kira's sister is in Ignarath. So are others. And what are we doing? Waiting for the Blade Council to decide the politics are convenient enough to mount a rescue."

I understood her anger. Felt it myself, burning in my chest alongside the food and the candlelight and the desperate attempt at normalcy. Vega was right. We were celebrating while others suffered. We were building lives while people died. The guilt of survival tasted like ash.

But I also knew that falling apart wouldn't help anyone.

"Vega." I kept my voice level. "Sit down."

"I don't—"

"Sit. Down."

She did, reluctantly, her jaw tight with frustration.

I looked around at the faces watching me. These women who'd followed me through hell and somehow come out the other side still breathing. They deserved honesty.

"You're right," I said. "We are celebrating while others suffer. We are building lives while people remain trapped. And yes, the politics are complicated, and the council is moving slowly."

"And?" Vega prompted, as if she wasn't *also* mated to a member of the council.

"And I don't fucking know," I snapped. "But ignoring the food in front of us isn't going to help the people in Ignarath. So let's eat our damn meals, and I'll talk to Darrokar. We're going to get them back. I promise."

I met the eyes of each of those women, even though Kira was the one who really needed to hear this. Vega had witnessed just how bad things were in Ignarath, people held as slaves, forced to fight in the arenas when they were no longer useful. We couldn't leave them there.

I just had no idea how or when we could really get them back.

I stuffed a bite of food in my mouth and chewed aggressively.

"Mom and Aunt Vega are fighting," Kaiya said. "It really *is* like Christmas back home."

Vega snorted, and the rest of us started laughing.

I'd take the win.

"TERRA, WAIT!" Eden's voice echoed through the corridor loud enough to make my ears ring.

I paused and looked over my shoulder. The air here was always warm, but tonight it felt stifling. I'd slipped out as the festivities were dying down. Lexa hadn't managed to coax Kira back but had assured us she was safe in her room. That was the best we could hope for.

For now.

"What's up, is everything alright?" Eden's face was flushed, her dark hair with its faded red high-lights sticking to her forehead. I would have been lying if I said I wasn't just a little more protective of Eden than of everyone else. She was the youngest, the most hopeful. Maybe the most adaptable among us.

This life was unlike what any of us had been promised, but she had the best chance at letting it all feel normal.

She caught up to me, panting slightly. She must have run the few hundred meters from the entrance to the human quarters. "I know we said no gifts, but …" She shoved a worn cloth bag at me.

The fabric was soft. When I opened it, the scent hit me first. Sweet, artificial, utterly Earth. Inside were maybe a dozen pieces of candy, wrapped in crinkled foil and plastic that had seen better days. Chocolate, hard candies, a piece of gum in a broken foil wrapper.

My throat tightened. Eden had been rationing this stash since we'd arrived, allowing herself maybe one piece every few weeks. I'd seen her unwrap them with the reverence other people reserved for religious artifacts.

"We said no gifts for a reason, kid, you didn't have to do this." But I didn't try to give it back. Couldn't. The gesture meant too much, even if it made something sharp twist in my chest.

Eden's mouth tightened fractionally, and I

winced internally. She hated being called kid. But, really, it was her own damn fault for being twenty years old.

"I just … you do so much for us. I thought you could use something sweet."

"Thank you." The words came out rougher than I'd intended. I tucked the bag into my jacket, close to my heart.

Something made the air shift. A change in pressure, in temperature. My training kicked in before conscious thought, every muscle in my body going tense. The sound reached us a heartbeat later: the heavy rush of wings cutting through air. I stepped in front of Eden without thinking, my hand moving instinctively toward the blade at my hip.

Two Drakarn dropped from the ceiling, their wings folding as they landed in crouches that spoke of barely contained violence. The first had scales the color of deep purple bruises, his yellow eyes fixed on us with obvious malice. The second was red as fresh blood, smaller but with the wiry build that suggested speed over strength.

I didn't recognize them by name, but I'd seen them in the training yards. Novice warriors, probably not much older than Eden, but still twice my size and armed with natural weapons I'd never possess.

My human flesh felt more exposed than ever.

"Eden, go home, now." My voice came out flat, commanding. Military.

"Yes, little softscale, go home," the purple one said, his voice a mockery of mine. His fangs gleamed in the light.

The red one flared his wings, the membrane throwing our shadows against the wall. "Run, little girl."

"Do it, Eden." I didn't take my eyes off them, but I was relieved to hear Eden's retreating footsteps. The sound faded quickly, swallowed by the stone corridors. Good. She didn't need to see this idiocy.

The purple one took a step closer, his claws clicking against the stone floor. "Look at this, Vareth. The human thinks she can stand against us."

"Pathetic," Vareth agreed. His tail lashed behind him like an angry cat's. "No scales, no claws, no wings. What are you going to do, soft thing? Bleed on us?"

They circled me slowly, testing, looking for weakness. This wasn't random harassment. This was calculated intimidation, designed to make me feel small and helpless. It might have worked if I hadn't spent the last eight months learning to survive in a world that wanted me dead.

"The Skalanth begins soon," the purple one continued, his voice taking on the tone of someone reciting scripture. "A time for true warriors to prove their worth. To bring honor to Scalvaris through strength and skill."

"Not like the cowards who hide behind their mates," Vareth added, his gaze raking over me with obvious disgust. "Real warriors earn their place through blood and victory."

"But the Warrior Lord's pet knows nothing of honor," Vareth said.

I resisted the urge to roll my eyes. This again. As if I hadn't heard it a hundred times before.

The accusation was tired and completely predictable. Darrokar's human mate, too weak to fight, too soft to belong, corrupting their perfect warrior society with my mere existence. I didn't give a single damn about their opinions, but apparently, they hadn't gotten the message.

"Challenge us," the purple one said, stepping closer. His breath was hot against my face, carrying the scent of smoke and sulfur. "Prove you belong here. Show us this honor you claim to possess."

"Unless you're too frightened," Vareth added with a sneer. "Too weak. Too *human*."

My hand tightened on my blade's hilt, but I didn't draw it. They wanted me to make the first move, to give them justification for what they planned to do anyway.

In Scalvaris, attacking an opponent unprovoked carried serious consequences, especially when that opponent was mated to the Warrior Lord. But if I drew first, if I made it a formal challenge, all bets were off.

And while I'd had months of practice, while I could hold my own against some of the Drakarn in training, two on one against warriors who'd been fighting since they could walk were not odds I was willing to chance. I wasn't suicidal.

The sound of running footsteps echoed through the corridor, human feet pounding against stone. Multiple sets, moving fast and with purpose. Relief flooded through me, followed immediately by worry. If my people got involved, this could escalate beyond anyone's control.

"What the fuck do you weasels want?" Vega demanded.

So much for diplomacy.

Lexa and Hawk flanked Vega, all armed and ready for violence. The dynamic in the corridor shifted instantly. Two on one had become two on four, and while the Drakarn still had physical advantages, we had numbers and the kind of desperate fury that came from months of suppressed frustration.

"Back off," Hawk said. "Now."

Lexa said nothing, but the knife in her hand caught the light, and her stance spoke of someone who knew how to use it.

The purple one's wings flared wider, a display of dominance that might have been impressive if he wasn't outnumbered. "Four soft things instead of one. How terrifying."

"Test us and find out," Vega said, her voice deadly calm. She'd positioned herself slightly ahead of the others, ready to take the first hit if it came to that. "I'm betting Darrokar won't be pleased if he finds out you've been harassing his mate."

And with Vega and Hawk there, add in Zarvash and Khorlar. Three males no Drakarn would want to cross.

That gave them pause. The red one's tail

stopped lashing, and I saw calculation flicker across his features. They might be young and stupid, but they weren't completely insane.

"Retreat to your mate," the purple one said, backing toward the ceiling. "The Skalanth will show everyone what real strength looks like."

"Looking forward to it," I said, my voice steady despite the adrenaline still coursing through my system.

They launched themselves upward with powerful wing beats, disappearing into the shadows above. The corridor fell silent except for the sound of our breathing and the distant hum of the mountain's geothermal systems.

"Me and Hawk will walk you home," said Vega. "It's on the way for us."

Lexa was still holding a wickedly sharp knife and staring at the ceiling above us. It was easy to forget we were living in caves sometimes, given how tall the ceilings could be. At moments like this, I cursed them. Too many places to hide, too many angles of attack. The Drakarn had all the advantages in their own territory.

"That's a good idea," Lexa agreed, finally sheathing her blade. "They don't bother us when we're at home."

Was that good enough? That the unmated humans could sleep without worrying about attack? Was that all they could hope for?

We'd survived eight months on this alien world, carved out a place for ourselves among warriors and politicians and fanatics who wanted us gone. I was starting to believe that we might actually have a future here.

But tonight was a reminder that acceptance was fragile, that there would always be those who saw us as invaders, as corruption, as something to be eliminated.

Things were supposed to get easier, the longer we survived here.

So why did it feel like it was only getting worse?

DARROKAR

TERRA SAT cross-legged on the floor near the bathing pool, her back to the entrance. Her blade lay across her knees, and she worked a whetstone along its edge with mechanical precision. The sound grated against my nerves, sharp and aggressive. Each stroke too hard, too fast, like she was trying to grind the metal down to nothing.

I stopped just inside the doorway and watched her.

The set of her shoulders told me everything. Every muscle in her back drawn tight enough to snap. Her knuckles were white where she gripped the blade's hilt, and the whetstone moved with barely controlled violence.

Something had happened.

I felt it in my chest, a tightness that had nothing to do with my own emotions and everything to do with hers. Fear. Anger. Both twisted together until I couldn't separate them.

My claws flexed. The urge to cross to her, to demand answers, to find whoever had put that tension in her spine and tear them apart, it burned through me. But I forced myself to stillness. She knew I was here. She'd heard me enter. And she was choosing not to acknowledge my presence.

That meant she needed space. Or she was trying to work through something on her own.

Or she was avoiding a conversation she didn't want to have.

I stayed where I was and let the silence stretch.

The blade sang against the stone. Over and over. A pattern she'd repeated so many times the sound had worn grooves into my patience.

"Tell me about the Skalanth," she said without looking up.

The question came out too carefully neutral. Like she'd been waiting for me to arrive so she could ask with exactly that tone.

I moved deeper into the quarters, my steps

loud enough that she could track my approach. "What do you want to know?"

"What it involves. Why it matters." Another stroke, harder than necessary. "You've been preparing for weeks. I should probably understand what all the fuss is about."

She was looking for something specific but approaching it sideways, like she thought I wouldn't notice.

I did.

I crossed the space between us and knelt behind her. Close enough that my body heat would reach her, that she'd feel my presence at her back. But I didn't touch her.

"It's a trial," I said. "For young warriors who want to prove themselves worthy of their rank."

"And they do this how?"

"By retrieving the blood-flame from the inner sanctum of the Forge Temple and delivering it to the waiting priests at the city's edge."

Her hands stilled on the blade. "It doesn't sound that complicated."

"It isn't. If you can get past the obstacles, the traps, and the senior warriors positioned between the sanctum and the finish." I let that sink in. "Most can't."

"What happens if they fail?" she was still working her blade.

"They try again next year. If they survive the attempt."

That got her attention. She turned her head slightly, not quite looking at me but acknowledging the weight of those words. "People die?"

"Sometimes. We do try to avoid it." I kept my voice level, factual. "Broken bones are common. Serious injuries happen. We do what we can to prevent deaths, but when you put young warriors in a situation designed to test their limits, the idiots will do their best to ruin it."

She set the blade down carefully. Too carefully. Like she was afraid if she moved too quickly, she'd do something she couldn't take back. "It sounds dangerous."

"It is."

"But important."

"Yes."

She picked up the whetstone again, turned it over in her hands. The motion was absent, distracted. Her mind was somewhere else entirely. "Maybe I should participate."

The suggestion struck me so hard it stole my breath.

"No." The refusal came out harder than I'd intended, but I didn't soften it. Couldn't. The very thought of Terra in the Skalanth, facing obstacles designed to challenge warriors twice her size with natural weapons she didn't possess, it made something violent and protective roar to life in my chest.

"It would be good training," she said, still not looking at me. "A chance to test myself against your warriors. Show them I'm not just some fragile human who needs protection at every turn."

"You have nothing to prove."

"Don't I?" She finally turned to face me, and the expression in her eyes made my fangs ache. "Half of Scalvaris thinks I'm corrupting you. That I'm weak. That I don't belong here. Maybe if I participated, proved I could handle myself by their standards, they'd—"

"They'd what?" I interrupted. "Accept you? Welcome you? Stop seeing you as an outsider?" I leaned closer, holding her gaze. "You could win the Skalanth outright, and there would still be those who resent your presence. Karyseth and her followers won't change their minds because you retrieve a sacred gem. They'll just find new reasons to justify their hatred."

"So I should do nothing? Just let them talk? Let them treat me like I'm some kind of parasite?"

"You should let me handle it." It was the wrong thing to say. I knew it the moment the words left my mouth.

Her expression shuttered. She turned back to her blade, picked it up, started working the whetstone again. "Right. Because that's what I do. Hide behind the Warrior Lord while he fights my battles."

"That's not what I meant."

"Isn't it?"

I could push. Demand she stop deflecting and tell me what had really happened. Use my size, my strength, my authority to force the conversation she was avoiding.

Instead, I reached out and took the blade from her hands.

She started to protest, but I set the weapon aside and shifted closer. My chest pressed against her back, my arms coming around her waist. I buried my face in her hair and breathed deep, letting her scent fill my lungs. Sweet. Wild.

Mine.

"Darrokar—"

"Later," I said against her neck. "We'll talk about the Skalanth later."

"We're talking about it now."

"No. We're not." I found the sensitive spot just below her ear and traced it with my tongue. Felt her shiver. Felt the tension in her spine shift from anger to something else entirely. "Right now, I'm going to distract you."

"I don't need to be distracted."

"Yes, you do." I moved my hands up her sides, slow and intentional, feeling the way her breathing changed when I reached her ribs. "You're wound tight enough to snap. Whatever happened, whatever you're not telling me, it's eating at you. So let me take your mind off it."

"That's not how this works."

"Of course it is." I turned her in my arms until she faced me, until I could see her eyes. "You're my mate. Your pain is mine. And if I can ease it, even temporarily, I will."

She opened her mouth to argue. I kissed her before she could.

The taste of her flooded my senses. Sweet. Soft. Everything opposite to the violence and stone and heat that defined my world. I gentled the kiss, kept it slow despite the urgency burning through my veins.

It wasn't about claiming or possessing.

It was about comfort. Connection. Reminding her that whatever had happened, whatever she was facing, she didn't face it alone.

She resisted for maybe three seconds. Then she melted into me with a sound that made my chest ache.

I took my time undressing her. My claws traced patterns on her skin as I exposed it, careful not to scratch, just to feel. The contrast between her softness and my scales never failed to undo something in me. She was so breakable. So fragile. And yet she'd survived everything this world had thrown at her.

She was stronger than anyone believed.

I picked her up and carried her to the center of the room, laying her back on our sleeping plat-form, the silks soft beneath her. The heat crystals cast her skin in warm light, made her hair look like flame against the dark material.

My cock twitched with want.

I covered her body with mine, careful of my weight, and kissed her again. Deeper this time. Tasting her thoroughly, loving the sounds she made when I found the spots that made her gasp. Her hands came up to grip my shoulders, nails digging in, and I growled my approval against her mouth.

"Darrokar." My name on her lips was a prayer. A plea.

"I have you, *luvae*." I moved down her body, trailing kisses along her throat, her collarbone, the soft skin between her breasts. "Let me take care of you."

I worshipped her with my mouth. Every inch of skin. Every curve and hollow. I learned the places that made her arch, the touches that made her whimper. My tail wound around her thigh, holding her open for me, and when I finally put my mouth on her pussy, she cried out loud enough to echo off the stone walls.

I took my time there too. Used my tongue, my lips, the careful edge of my fangs to drive her higher. Licked through her folds, circled her clit, tasted how wet she was for me.

She tasted like salt and sweetness and desperation. Her hands fisted in my hair, holding me against her cunt, and I felt the moment she stopped thinking and surrendered completely to sensation.

When she came, it was with my name on her lips and her body trembling beneath my hands.

I gentled her through it, soft kisses and careful touches, until her breathing steadied. Then I moved back up her body and positioned myself between her thighs. The head of my cock pressed against her entrance, already slick from my body's natural preparation and her own wetness.

"Look at me," I said.

She did. Those green eyes met mine, hazy with pleasure but focused. Present.

I pushed in slowly. Watched her face as I filled her, as her sex stretched to accommodate me. The pleasure was intense, overwhelming, but I kept my movements controlled. It wasn't about taking. It was about giving. About showing her without words what she meant to me.

My length dragged against her inner walls, and the flexible tip curled to stroke the spots I'd learned drove her wild. She gasped, her nails digging into my shoulders hard enough to draw blood. The small pain only heightened the pleasure.

I set a rhythm. Slow. Deep. Each thrust intentional, designed to build her pleasure gradually instead of rushing toward the peak. My cock filled her completely, stretched her around me until I could feel every clench of her inner muscles. My tail wrapped around her leg, holding her steady, while my hands framed her face. I wanted to see every expression, every flicker of pleasure that crossed her features.

"You're mine," I said, the words falling from me without conscious thought. "Nothing changes that. Not tradition, not politics, not the opinions of fools who can't see your worth."

She opened her mouth to respond, but I angled my hips and hit the spot that made her lose her words. She arched beneath me with a cry that went straight to my cock.

"That's it," I encouraged. "Take what you need from me."

I increased the pace slightly, still controlled but with more force behind each thrust. The sound of our bodies joining filled the quarters, obscene and perfect. The wet slide of my cock into her, the slap of skin against scales. Her scent surrounded me, thick with arousal and satisfaction. The mate-bond sang between us, pleasure feeding back and forth until I couldn't tell where mine ended and hers began.

When she came the second time, it was

harder. Her entire body locked up, clenching around my cock with enough force to make me see stars. I followed her over with a roar, my cock pulsing as I came inside her, filling her with my cum while that clever tip continued to stroke, drawing out both our pleasure until we were both shaking.

I collapsed beside her, careful not to crush her, and pulled her against my chest. She came willingly, tucking herself into the curve of my body like she belonged there.

Because she did.

My tail wrapped around her calf. My wing draped over us both, creating a cocoon of warmth and safety. Her head rested over my heart, and I felt her breathing slow, steadying as the aftershocks faded.

For a while, we just lay there. No words. No need.

Then she stirred.

"I think I should do it. The Skalanth."

My hand stilled on her back. "Terra."

"Hear me out." She pushed up on her elbow to look at me. "I'm not saying I'd win. I know I wouldn't. But participating, showing that I'm willing to subject myself to the same trials the warriors face, that would mean something. Wouldn't it?"

"It would mean you're reckless."

"Or brave."

"Bravery and stupidity often look the same." I sat up, forcing her to move with me. "You're talking about entering a competition designed for Drakarn warriors. You don't have wings to navigate the vertical sections. You don't have our strength to break through barriers. You don't have scales to protect you when you fall."

"I have training. Skill. Intelligence."

"Which won't matter when a warrior twice your size knocks you off a wall. You could *die*."

"People die crossing the street back on Earth."

"This isn't Earth. And you're not just anyone. You're my mate. The Warrior Lord's consort. If something happened to you—" I cut myself off before I could finish that thought. Before I could voice the violence that would follow if she was harmed. "You've already proven yourself. A dozen times over."

"To you. To the humans. Maybe to some of the Blade Council." She shook her head. "But not to the traditionalists. Not to the warriors who see me as weakness. Not to Karyseth and her followers who think I'm corrupting everything they hold sacred."

"Their opinions don't matter."

"They do if they affect how I'm treated. How my *people* are treated." She moved away from me, putting distance between us. "You can protect me from direct threats. But you can't protect me from being dismissed, from being seen as less than, from being treated like I'm only here because of who I'm mated to instead of who I am."

The words hit harder than they should have. Because she was right. I could kill anyone who tried to harm her. Could destroy anyone who threatened her directly. But I couldn't change minds. Couldn't force respect or acceptance.

"The Skalanth won't change that," I said.

"Maybe not. But I need to try something." She wrapped her arms around herself, a defensive gesture that made my chest ache.

"No," I said.

"No?"

"I'm not agreeing to this. Not tonight. Not without more thought." I stood from the platform and crossed to where she'd left her blade and picked it up. The edge was sharp enough to split stone. "Whatever brought this on, whatever happened to make you think participating in the Skalanth is necessary, we're going to talk about it. Really talk about it. Not dance around it or deflect or seduce each other into forgetting the conversation."

She looked away. "Nothing happened."

"*Luvae*."

"I'm serious. Nothing worth mentioning."

I set the blade down and moved back to her. Caught her shoulders gently, waited until she looked at me. "I thought we were done keeping secrets."

Something flickered across her face. Guilt. Anger. Fear. It was gone too quickly to name, but I felt it through the bond like ice in my chest.

"It was nothing," she said again, but her voice was quieter now. Less certain.

"Tell me anyway."

She pulled away from my grip, moved to where her clothes lay scattered on the floor. She started dressing with sharp, jerky movements. "A couple of novice warriors were idiots. On my way back from the human quarters. They wanted to make a point about how I don't belong here. It's not the first time. It won't be the last. I handled it."

Each word landed like a blow.

Novice warriors. Confronting my mate. Making her feel unwelcome. *Threatening* her.

The rage that flooded through me was immediate and absolute. My vision narrowed. My wings flared. The urge to hunt, to find these fools and tear them apart for daring to approach her, it consumed every rational thought.

"Who?" The word came out as a growl, barely recognizable as language.

"It doesn't matter."

"Their names. Now."

"I don't know their names." She pulled her shirt over her head, still not looking at me. "I didn't exactly stop to exchange introductions."

"Describe them."

"Darrokar …"

"Describe them." I was moving before I'd made the conscious decision, heading for the door, ready to tear through Scalvaris until I found the warriors stupid enough to threaten what was mine.

She caught my arm. Small hands on my forearm, not enough strength to actually stop me but enough to make me pause.

"Don't," she said. "Please."

"They threatened you."

"They talked. That's all. Just words." She stepped in front of me, blocking the door. "If you go after them, you prove them right. You prove that I can't handle myself, that I need you to fight my battles, that I'm exactly as weak as they think I am."

"You're not weak."

"Then let me prove it." Her grip on my arm tightened. "Let me handle this myself. Let me show them that I can stand on my own without the Warrior Lord rushing to my defense every time someone says something I don't like."

"This is more than words. This is harassment. Intimidation."

"This is politics." She moved closer, her body pressing against mine. "And if you retaliate, it becomes a bigger problem. The traditionalists will say you're choosing me over Scalvaris. That you're willing to punish warriors for speaking their minds. That I've corrupted your judgment."

I knew she was right. Hated it, but knew it. If I hunted down these novices, if I made an example of them, it would only fuel the narrative that Terra was a weakness. A distraction. Something that made me unfit to lead.

But knowing she was right didn't cool the rage burning through my veins.

"I want names," I said. "Descriptions. Everything you remember."

"Why? So you can track them down later?"

"So I know who to watch. Who to keep away from you." I caught her face in my hands, careful of my claws. "I won't hunt them. Not unless they approach you again. But I'm not going to pretend this didn't happen."

She searched my eyes, looking for something. A promise I wasn't sure I could make.

"One was purple," she finally said. "Dark purple scales, yellow eyes. The other was red. Smaller. Faster-looking."

Purple and red. Novices. That narrowed it down to maybe two dozen warriors currently in training. Not enough to identify them specifically, but enough to start watching.

"Did they touch you?"

"No."

"Threaten you directly?"

"They implied things. They talked about the Skalanth." She paused. "That's where I got the idea."

So the whole conversation, her sudden interest

in participating, it all stemmed from a confrontation she'd tried to hide from me. Warriors had challenged her, had made her feel like she needed to prove herself, and instead of coming to me immediately, she'd sat alone, sharpening her blade and building walls.

The thought made something crack in my chest.

"You should have told me," I said. "Right away. The moment you got back."

"I handled it."

"That's not the point." I pulled her closer, needing the contact, needing to feel her safe against me. "You are my mate. That means when something happens, when someone threatens you, I need to know. Not because I think you can't handle yourself, but because your safety matters to me more than anything else in this world."

"And that's the problem." She pressed her forehead against my chest. "Your need to protect me, it's going to smother me if we're not careful. I can't live my life worrying that every challenge I face will send you into a protective rage."

"Then don't get challenged."

She laughed, but it was bitter. "That's not how this works. I'm human in Scalvaris. I'm mated to the Warrior Lord. I'm everything that some assholes in this city hate wrapped up in one very breakable package. The challenges aren't going to stop."

I knew that. Had known it from the moment I'd claimed her. But knowing something intellectually and facing it in practice were different things.

"I'm asking you not to participate in the Skalanth," I said.

She pulled back to look at me. "Are you ordering me?"

"Would it matter if I was?"

"No."

I'd expected that answer. Still hated hearing it.

"Then I'm asking," I said. "As your mate. Not as Warrior Lord. I'm asking you not to risk yourself this way."

She kissed me then, soft and sweet, and I tasted apology in it. Or maybe understanding. She pulled me back toward the sleeping platform, and I went willingly.

No one touched my mate.

Except me.

I FOUND Vega in one of the smaller training chambers, the kind tucked away in Scalvaris's maze of corridors where you had to know it existed to find it. She preferred these spaces. Quieter. Less crowded. No audience of Drakarn warriors watching her every move and making judgments.

She was running drills when I arrived. Endurance work, the kind that looked deceptively simple until you tried it yourself. Sprint to the wall, touch it, sprint back. Over and over until your lungs burned and your legs turned to jelly.

I watched her complete three cycles before she noticed me.

"You here to train or spectate?" she called without breaking stride.

"I thought I'd watch you sweat."

She rolled her eyes. "Get your ass out here."

I dropped my jacket and joined her. The first sprint felt good, muscles warming, blood pumping. The second was harder. By the fifth, I remembered why I usually avoided Vega's training sessions. The woman was relentless.

We ran in silence for a while. Just breathing and footfalls and the scrape of boots on stone. As usual, this place felt like a furnace. Sweat soaked through my shirt.

Finally, Vega slowed to a stop. She bent over, hands on knees, sucking air. I did the same, grateful for the break.

"So," she said between breaths. "What do you want?"

"Can't I just want to train with a friend?"

"You could. But you don't." She straightened, wiping sweat from her face. "You've got that look. The one that means you're about to do something stupid and you want someone to tell you it's a good idea."

Damn. She knew me too well.

I grabbed her water flask and took a long

drink, buying time and ignoring the faintly disgusted look she gave me for stealing her drink. "I'm thinking about entering the Skalanth."

Vega's expression didn't change. "No."

"You didn't even let me explain."

"I don't need to. The answer is no." She snatched the flask from me and took a drink. "That's a terrible idea."

Okay, this was not going as expected. "It would show them I can compete on their level."

"It would show them you're willing to break your neck for their approval." Vega's voice was flat. Final. "Which you shouldn't be."

I felt my jaw tighten. "I thought you'd understand."

"I do understand. That's why I'm saying no." She moved closer, her gray eyes sharp. "You're never going to win if you play by their rules, Terra. The whole fucking thing is rigged. It's designed for Drakarn warriors for Drakarn strengths. You entering doesn't prove you're strong. It proves you're desperate."

The word hit harder than it should have.

"I'm not desperate."

"Then why are you considering this?" Vega gestured at the training chamber around us.

"You've already proven yourself. Multiple times. You led the defense when those desert predators attacked. You've trained with their warriors and held your own. You survived a crash landing on an alien planet and built a life here. What more do you need to prove?"

"That I belong," I said quietly. *With Darrokar.* I couldn't bring myself to say that last bit out loud. I *did.* He was my mate. Fate had decreed it, and the rest of the universe could take a hike.

"To whom? Karyseth? The fuckers who hate us on principle?" Vega shook her head. "They're never going to accept you. Not if you win the Skalanth. Not if you single-handedly save the city. They've decided you're the enemy, and nothing you do will change that."

"So I should just accept the bullshit? Let them treat me like I'm some kind of parasite?"

"No. You should stop caring what they think." Vega's voice softened slightly. "The Skalanth is about pride. Tradition. It's not about real worth or actual capability. It's a ritual designed to reinforce their hierarchy and their values. Why do you need validation from a system that was never built for you?"

I wanted to argue. Wanted to explain that it

was more complicated than that, that my position as Darrokar's mate meant I had to meet certain expectations, that proving myself wasn't about validation but about survival.

But the words stuck in my throat.

"What does Zarvash think?" I asked instead. Her own mate had once been one of the traditionalists opposed to our presence. Despite his relationship with Vega, I thought he still had a few lingering doubts about us humans.

Vega's mouth twitched. "About the Skalanth? He thinks it's a useful tradition that serves a purpose for Drakarn society. About entering it?" She paused. "We've discussed it. He agrees with me."

That surprised me. "Really?"

"Really." Vega leaned against the wall, her posture relaxing slightly. "Zarvash is pragmatic. He understands that humans and Drakarn have different strengths. He doesn't expect me to compete in their trials any more than I expect him to, I don't know, pilot a spaceship or something. We bring different things to the table."

"But you're not mated to the Warrior Lord."

"No. I'm mated to his Strategic Advisor." Vega's eyes narrowed. "Which means I deal with plenty of political bullshit myself. And I've learned that trying to meet impossible expectations is a waste of energy. Focus on what you're actually good at, not what they think you should be good at."

I turned away, frustration building in my chest. "Easy for you to say."

"Is it?" Her voice had an edge now. "You think I don't get challenged? That warriors don't question why Zarvash chose a human? I get plenty of shit. I just don't let it dictate my choices."

"Because you don't have to." The words came out sharper than I'd intended. "You're not the Warrior Lord's consort. You're not the visible symbol of human-Drakarn relations. When people look at you, they see *you*. When they look at me, they see Darrokar's weakness."

Silence fell between us.

Vega studied me for a long moment. Then she sighed. "You're right. Your position is different. The scrutiny is worse. But that doesn't make the Skalanth a good idea. If anything, it makes it worse. You fail, and it confirms everything they believe about humans being weak. You succeed, and they'll say you cheated or that the trials were made easier for you. There's no winning move here."

I knew she was right. Hated it but knew it.

"So what do I do?" I asked. "Just keep taking the harassment? Keep letting them treat me like I don't belong?"

"You keep doing what you've been doing. Living your life. Doing your work. Being competent and capable and refusing to apologize for existing." Vega pushed off the wall. "We can't win them all over. Some people are always going to hate us. But we don't need everyone's approval to build a life here. We just need enough people to see our worth. And you've already got that."

She was making sense. I didn't want her to be making sense, but she was.

"I need to think," I said.

"Good. Think hard. And when you're done thinking, come to the same conclusion I already reached." Vega grabbed her jacket. "Don't do the Skalanth. It's not worth it."

She left me alone in the training chamber.

I stood there for a while, sweat cooling on my skin, listening to the distant sounds of Scalvaris. Voices echoing through corridors. The rush of the underground river. The ever-present hum of geothermal vents.

Vega was right. I *knew* she was right.

But knowing something and accepting it were different things.

I grabbed my jacket and headed out, no clear destination in mind. Just walking. Letting my feet carry me through the familiar passages while my brain spun in circles.

The market district sprawled ahead of me before I'd consciously decided to go there. The scent hit me first. Spices and smoke and something sweet I couldn't identify. Then the sounds. Vendors calling out their wares, customers haggling, the general chaos of commerce.

I wove through the crowd, human-small among the towering Drakarn bodies. Most ignored me. A few nodded in acknowledgment. One vendor tried to sell me something that looked like dried meat but smelled like sulfur. I politely declined.

Then I saw Orla.

She sat in a small courtyard just off the main market flow, cross-legged on the ground with some kind of device spread out in front of her. Tools scattered around her. Her hands moved quickly, adjusting something, tightening something else.

Three Drakarn children clustered nearby, watching with open curiosity.

I stopped at the courtyard's edge, half-hidden behind a pillar.

"What does it do?" one of the children asked. Young, maybe eight or nine. Her scales were bright green.

"It measures heat signatures," Orla said without looking up. "See this part here? It detects changes in temperature and converts them to visual data."

"Why?"

"Because sometimes you need to find things that are warmer or cooler than their surroundings. Like tracking someone through a tunnel system. Or finding a heat vent that's about to fail."

The child leaned closer. "Can I touch it?"

"Gently." Orla guided the small clawed hand to a safe part of the device. "Feel that? That's the sensor array. Very delicate."

The child touched it with surprising care. Her eyes widened. "It's warm."

"That's because it's active. Reading the ambient temperature right now." Orla made another adjustment and held up the device. "Want to see it work?"

All three children crowded closer.

I watched Orla demonstrate her invention, explaining the technical details in terms the children could understand. They asked questions. She answered patiently. No defensiveness. No need to prove herself. Just a scientist sharing her work with curious minds.

Footsteps approached from behind me. I glanced back and saw Selene, Reika, and Kinsley heading toward the courtyard. They hadn't noticed me yet.

I stepped back, deeper into the shadow of the pillar.

Selene reached Orla first. "Making friends?"

"Educating the next generation," Orla corrected with a grin.

Reika hung back slightly, her posture still uncertain around strangers. But Kinsley moved forward confidently, kneeling down to the children's level.

"That's a clever design," she said, examining Orla's device.

One of the children, the green-scaled girl, looked at Reika. "Are you scared?"

Everyone went still.

Reika's hands twisted together. But she met the child's eyes. "Sometimes. But I'm learning to be brave."

"My mama says being brave means doing things even when you're scared."

"Your mama is very wise."

The child beamed.

I watched the four women interact with the Drakarn children. Natural. Easy. No one was challenging them. No one was questioning their right to be there. They were just people, sharing space, existing together.

They weren't trying to prove anything.

They were just living.

A Drakarn adult approached the courtyard, probably a parent collecting their child. She nodded to the humans with casual politeness. "Thank you for entertaining them."

"Our pleasure," Selene said.

The adult gathered her children and left. The courtyard quieted.

I stayed in my hiding spot, watching.

Orla packed up her device with careful movements. Reika had relaxed slightly, her shoulders not quite so hunched. Selene stood guard, not obviously, just aware of their surroundings in that way healers learned.

They looked like they belonged.

Not because they'd proven themselves in some grand trial. Not because they'd won over every skeptic. Just because they'd carved out a space and filled it with their presence.

The pressure I felt, the constant need to justify my existence, to prove I was worthy of Darrokar's choice, that was unique to me. The other women weren't immune to harassment or prejudice. But they also weren't carrying the weight of being the Warrior Lord's mate.

Every decision I made reflected on Darrokar. Every failure confirmed the traditionalists' beliefs. Every success was attributed to his protection rather than my capability.

I was trying to meet expectations that were impossible by design.

But I couldn't leave Darrokar. Wouldn't. The mate bond aside, I loved him. Loved the life we were building together. Loved the future we could create.

So what was the solution?

I didn't know.

I turned away from the courtyard before my

friends could spot me. Walked back through the market, through the corridors, letting my feet carry me without conscious direction.

Vega said the Skalanth wasn't the answer, but I couldn't make myself agree. Failing a trial designed for Drakarn strengths would bruise my pride.

But what if I didn't fail?

What if I showed them …

Something.

Darrokar might actually kill me if I tried it. He'd wanted me to promise to stay away. And I hadn't, not exactly.

Though that was almost a lie. I'd deflected when I should have been honest, hidden when I should have told the truth. And I still didn't know what to do.

I only had a day to decide. Excited whispers whipped through the city as everyone prepared for the festivities.

No one expected me to do it.

No one would judge me for sitting out any more than they judged me for existing.

I kept walking through town and hoped an answer would come to me.

7

DARROKAR

THE BLOOD-FLAME PULSED in its cradle. I stood with my back to the chamber's entrance, wings folded tight, every muscle locked in the stillness that came from hours of guard duty. Rath flanked my left. Nyx held the right, gray as stone and just as immovable.

One hour until the Skalanth officially began.

One hour until novice warriors would attempt to breach the sanctum, navigate the traps and obstacles we'd designed, and claim the blood-flame for themselves. Most would fail. Some would get injured. A few might actually make it this far, only to face the three of us blocking their path.

It was tradition. Sacred. The kind of duty that demanded full attention and unwavering focus.

So why couldn't I stop thinking about Terra?

I hadn't seen her since dawn. She'd been gone when I woke, her side of the sleeping platform already cold. Not unusual. She often rose early to train or meet with the other humans. But something about her absence this morning felt different. Secretive.

My claws flexed against my palms.

"You're thinking too loud," Rath said without turning his head.

"I'm not thinking anything."

"This will be fine." He shifted his weight, tail swaying slightly. "We stand here awhile, hold off the younglings, and then return triumphant to our mates," he glanced at Nyx, "or an empty cot."

Nyx made a rude gesture.

Rath was right. We simply had to wait it out, and then I could find Terra and figure out what was going on.

I forced my attention back to the sanctum. The blood-flame sat in its cradle on the sacred podium. The chamber remained empty except for us. Everything was exactly as it should be.

Except for the growing unease crawling up my spine.

Our conversation played through my mind on repeat. Terra asking about the Skalanth. Suggesting she participate. Me refusing. Her kissing me instead of arguing, which should have been my first warning that she hadn't actually agreed to anything.

"I told her not to come," I said, half to myself.

She wouldn't.

Would she?

"And your mate will do as commanded," Rath said, his tone casual. Too casual.

The words hung in the air.

Silence stretched between the three of us, heavy and damning.

Then Nyx turned his head, slow and steady, to look at me. His expression said everything his mouth didn't need to.

"Hells," I breathed.

Before Rath could make another jab, footsteps echoed from the corridor outside. A young messenger, barely past his novice trials, skidded to a halt at the sanctum entrance. His chest heaved, scales flushed dark with exertion. He had his wings held in tight to his back and looked a bit overawed to be in front of me.

"Warrior Lord." He bowed, nearly losing his balance. "A message from Commander Khorlar."

My spine locked. Khorlar wouldn't send a messenger unless something had gone catastrophically wrong. Was it Ignarath? We didn't war over the sacred holidays, but I wouldn't put any treachery past them.

"Speak."

The youth straightened, held out a slip of paper. His claws trembled as he extended it. "The Commander said it was urgent, my lord. That you'd want to know immediately."

Khorlar's sharp script cut across the page in three damning lines: *Your mate joined the blessing ceremony with the other warriors. She's entering the Skalanth.*

Ice flooded my veins.

"No." The word came out flat. "No, she wouldn't."

Gods damn it.

"Hells." I crumpled the message in my fist. "*Damnation!*"

The messenger flinched back.

Rath moved closer, reading over my shoulder.

His expression shifted. Confusion, then understanding, then grim resignation.

"Well," he said carefully, "at least now we know where she is."

The truth washed over me. Terra was entering the Skalanth. Despite what we'd said. Despite my warnings. Soon, she'd be in the maze of corridors and traps.

My mate was competing against warriors twice her size with advantages she'd never possess.

I was moving before I'd made the conscious decision, wings spreading, ready to launch myself toward the exit.

Rath's hand caught my shoulder. "Don't."

"She's out there."

"I know."

"Alone. Vulnerable. Facing gods know what obstacles and warriors who already hate her." My voice came out as a snarl, barely recognizable. "I'm not standing here while she risks her neck for their approval."

"Yes, you are." Rath's grip tightened, claws digging in just enough to ground me. "Because abandoning your post one hour before the trials begin will give Karyseth exactly what she wants."

"I don't give a single damn about what Kary-seth wants."

"You should." Rath moved to block my path entirely, his bulk filling the space between me and the exit. "Those yellow-robed priests are every-where today. Watching. Waiting for any excuse to claim you're unfit to lead. That your human has messed up your judgment. That you value her over Scalvaris itself."

"*I do.*"

Nyx hissed at that, but neither he nor Rath argued.

"She could die crossing the market on any given day. It didn't stop you from letting her have freedom before." His eyes held mine, hard and uncompromising. "This is no different, and you know it. This is her choice. Her risk. And if you interfere, you undermine her every effort. This would be for *nothing.*"

The logic was sound. I still growled.

"Besides," Rath continued, his voice softening slightly, "you storming out there won't help the larger mission. We need political capital for the Ignarath rescue. The Council's barely agreed to consider it after the Skalanth concludes. You cause a scene now, abandon your sacred duty for your mate, and that approval disappears. Along with any chance of reminding Ignarath of their place."

Rath was right. Damn him, but he was right.

I looked at Nyx. I would be missed. He wouldn't be. Not here, not now. "Go. Shadow her," I said. "Don't interfere unless absolutely necessary. But keep her alive."

"Understood." Nyx paused at the threshold to the entrance. "She's stronger than you think."

"I know exactly how strong she is. That's not the problem."

He left without another word, disappearing into the corridors beyond.

I turned back to the blood-flame, forcing myself to resume my position. To stand guard like nothing had changed. Like my mate wasn't somewhere in this mountain, ready to face trials designed to break Drakarn warriors.

Rath settled back into his own stance. "She'll be fine."

"You don't know that."

"No. But I know Terra. She doesn't do anything without a plan." He was quiet for a moment. "Even if that plan is going to give you gray scales."

"I don't have gray scales."

"Give it an hour."

The attempt at humor fell flat. I couldn't find it in me to laugh, couldn't pretend this was anything other than torture. Every instinct I possessed screamed at me to hunt, to find her, to eliminate any threat before it could touch her.

Instead, I stood in a sacred chamber and waited.

Time crawled.

My claws flexed rhythmically, the only outlet I allowed myself. My tail lashed once, twice, before I forced it still. Wings wanted to spread, to carry me through these corridors until I found her. I kept them folded through sheer will.

"Why would she do this?" The question escaped before I could stop it.

Rath didn't pretend to misunderstand. "Because she's trying to survive in a world that wasn't built for her. Because she's tired of being seen as your weakness. Because she's probably a little bit insane."

"She has nothing to prove."

"To you, maybe. To herself?" Rath shrugged. "That's different."

I thought about the novice warriors who'd

confronted her. The ones she'd tried to hide from me. The constant pressure of being the Warrior Lord's mate, of representing all humans to a population that largely wished they didn't exist.

She was trying to claim space in a world determined to deny her.

I understood it. And I wished I could change this world so she never had to worry. But a Warrior Lord's power only stretched so far.

"If she gets hurt," I said quietly, "I'm going to tear apart every warrior who laid a claw on her."

"Fair enough." Rath's tone was mild. "Can you wait until after we get the agreement to attack Ignarath?"

"I'll consider it."

He snorted. As if Rath was any more sane when it came to his own mate. He'd been lucky she was no warrior.

The sanctum fell silent again.

Somewhere in the labyrinth beyond, Terra would soon be fighting. Climbing. Surviving. Proving herself to people who would never see her worth no matter what she accomplished.

And I was stuck here, playing my role, maintaining my position, being the Warrior Lord instead of the mate who wanted to burn down anything that threatened her.

Nyx would keep her safe. I had to trust that. Had to believe in his skill and his judgment and Terra's own capability.

But trust didn't make the waiting easier.

My claws flexed again.

One hour until the Skalanth began.

One hour of not knowing if my mate was safe.

One hour of forced stillness while everything in me demanded action.

One hour of understanding exactly why Terra had done this, even as I wanted to lock her in our quarters and never let her face danger again.

"She's going to be insufferable if she succeeds," Rath observed.

"She's already insufferable."

"You love it."

I did. And I couldn't stop from grinning.

The waiting continued.

My fury simmered.

I couldn't believe she'd done something this stupid.

Except I knew my mate. And, of course she had.

8

TERRA

THE GATHERING SQUARE at the river's edge was packed with Drakarn bodies. Massive and scaled and radiating heat like living furnaces. I stood among them, human-small and feeling every inch of the difference. My palms were slick with sweat despite the heat.

This was possibly the stupidest thing I'd ever done.

And I willingly slept with a seven-foot-tall alien warrior, claws and wings every night, so the bar was high.

The underground river rushed past the square's eastern edge, its surface glowing faintly from the algae that clung to the rocks below. The sound of it filled the space, a constant roar that should have been soothing but instead it was amplifying every anxious thought in my skull.

I smoothed my palm over the blade at my hip. The leather wrapping on the hilt was worn smooth from use, familiar under my fingers. It helped. A little.

Around me, Drakarn warriors stretched and tested their weapons. Wings flared and folded. Tails lashed. Claws flexed. They moved with the kind of casual confidence that came from a lifetime of knowing exactly what their bodies could do. Knowing they belonged here.

I didn't belong here.

Not like I had a choice.

The decision had felt clearer last night. Lying awake while Darrokar slept, running through every conversation, every slight, every moment of being dismissed or challenged or treated like I was only relevant because of who I'd mated. The Skalanth had seemed like the answer. A way to prove I could compete on their terms, in their world, by their rules.

Now, standing in a crowd of warriors who could break me in half without trying, the clarity had given way to something closer to panic.

What the hell was I thinking?

A purple-scaled warrior to my left glanced down at me. His yellow eyes narrowed, and his lip curled just enough to show fang. Recognition flickered across his features. One of the novices who'd cornered me in the corridor. He opened his mouth, probably to say something he thought was clever, but a larger warrior shouldered past him, and the moment broke.

I exhaled slowly through my nose.

Focus. I was here. I'd made the choice. Second-guessing it now wouldn't help.

The crowd shifted, bodies pressing closer as more warriors arrived. I got jostled by a wing, nearly knocked sideways by a tail. No one apologized. Most didn't even notice. To them, I was just another obstacle to navigate around.

Or maybe they noticed and didn't care. Now was the perfect opportunity to get a hit in on the Warrior Lord's mate without any consequences.

Darrokar was going to lose his mind when he realized what I was doing.

I'd left before dawn, slipping out of our quarters while he still slept. Cowardly, maybe. But I couldn't face the argument I knew would come. Couldn't risk him talking me out of this or, worse, trying to forbid it outright. He was still figuring out how to deal with a headstrong human, one who didn't follow his every order like it was his right to issue it.

"Finally, there you are."

I turned at the familiar voice and found Lexa pushing through the crowd toward me. Her blonde hair was pulled back in a tight braid, and she wore the kind of practical fighting leathers we'd scrounged from the Scalvaris markets. A knife hung at each hip, and her expression was caught somewhere between exasperation and resignation.

"What are you doing here?" I asked.

"Helping to keep you alive." She stopped beside me, close enough that her shoulder brushed mine. The contact was reassuring.

Guilt twisted in my chest. "Lexa—"

"Save it." She cut me off with a sharp gesture. "We can argue about your choices later. We're here now."

"We?"

"You think I'm letting you do this alone?" Lexa's mouth twitched. "You've been champing at the bit to do something idiotic since those two assholes gave you trouble. You need someone to back you up."

Before I could respond, another voice joined us.

"Make that two someones."

Vega appeared on my other side. She looked calm. Too calm. The kind of calm that meant she was furious but had decided to channel it into something productive.

"I thought you said this was a bad idea," I said.

"It's a very bad idea." Vega's gray eyes met mine, hard and uncompromising. "But you were always going to do it anyway, so here we are."

"I didn't ask you to come."

"Good thing I don't need your permission." She shifted her weight, settling into a ready stance. "I've done enough stupid things in my life. Figured I owe you backup for at least one of yours."

The tightness in my chest eased slightly. I hadn't asked for help. Hadn't wanted to drag anyone else into this mess. But having Lexa and Vega flanking me, solid and present and ready to fight, it made the impossible feel slightly less insane.

"Thank you," I said quietly.

"Don't thank us yet." Lexa's gaze swept the

assembled warriors. "We might all regret this in about ten minutes."

"Optimistic," Vega muttered. "I'm giving it five."

A hush fell over the square.

The crowd parted, bodies shifting to create a path. Karyseth emerged from the corridor beyond, her golden scales gleaming like coins in firelight. She wore ceremonial robes, deep red fabric that pooled around her feet and trailed behind her as she walked. Other priests followed in her wake, their own yellow robes marking them as temple initiates.

The air grew thick with incense. Sweet and cloying, it caught in my throat and made my eyes water. The priests carried censers that swung on chains, smoke pouring from the perforated metal in gray-white clouds.

Karyseth's gaze swept the assembled warriors. Assessing. Judging. Her expression was serene, almost peaceful, which somehow made her more terrifying than if she'd been openly hostile.

Then her eyes found me.

Everything in me went still.

She looked at me for a long moment. Long enough that the warriors nearby noticed. Long enough that whispers started rippling through the crowd. Her expression didn't change. No surprise. No anger. Just that same terrible calm.

I waited for her to object. To declare that humans had no place in the Skalanth. To use this moment to humiliate me in front of half of Scalvaris.

She didn't.

Instead, she held my gaze for another heartbeat, then continued her scan of the crowd as if I was no more noteworthy than any other participant.

"We can still leave," Lexa said quietly. "No shame in changing your mind."

I could. The thought was tempting. Turn around, walk out of this square, go back to Darrokar and admit I'd been an idiot. Face his anger and his relief and his overprotective fury.

But then what?

The harassment would continue. The challenges. The constant pressure of being seen as weakness incarnate. Nothing would change except I'd have confirmed that I couldn't handle their world.

"I'm staying," I said.

Vega sighed. "Yeah, that tracks."

Karyseth raised her hands, and the crowd fell silent. Even the river seemed to quiet, though I knew that was just my imagination. She began to speak, her voice carrying across the square with the kind of projection that came from years of public ritual.

"Warriors of Scalvaris." The words rolled out, formal and weighted. "You stand at the threshold of the Skalanth. A trial as old as this city. A test of strength, cunning, and honor."

The assembled warriors straightened. Pride radiated from them.

"The blood-flame awaits in the Temple's inner sanctum." Karyseth's hands moved in patterns I didn't understand, probably some kind of blessing. "Your task is simple. Retrieve the sacred gem. Carry it through the city. Deliver it to the waiting priest at Scalvaris's edge before the suns reach their zenith."

Simple. Right. If you ignored the obstacles, the traps, and the senior warriors who'd be actively trying to stop us.

"The warrior who succeeds will lead the victory procession. Will be honored before the Blade Council. Will prove themselves worthy of Scalvaris's highest regard."

More than a few warriors puffed up at that. Glory. Recognition. The kind of status that could define a career.

I just wanted to survive.

"The rules are thus," Karyseth continued. "Killing is forbidden. Any warrior who takes a life will be punished. Captured participants will be marked with ash and are honor-bound to withdraw. Once you leave this square, the senior warriors will hunt you. They will test you. They will push you to your limits."

She paused, letting that sink in.

"But they will not break you. Not if you are truly worthy."

The incense smoke swirled thicker. The priests began chanting, low and rhythmic. The sound vibrated through the stone beneath my feet, through my bones.

Karyseth's gaze found me again. Just for a moment. Just long enough for me to see the cold calculation in her eyes.

She wanted me to fail. Wanted everyone to see. Wanted proof that humans couldn't compete.

Fine.

I'd give her a show.

The chanting reached a crescendo, then cut

off abruptly. Silence crashed down, heavy and expectant.

"When the horn sounds," Karyseth said, "the Skalanth begins. May the strongest prevail. May the worthy triumph. May Scalvaris be honored by your efforts."

She stepped back. One of the priests raised a horn to his lips, the instrument carved from some kind of bone and polished until it gleamed.

This was it.

No going back now.

I checked my blade one more time. Made sure my boots were laced tight. Rolled my shoulders to loosen the tension that had locked my muscles.

Beside me, Lexa shifted her weight onto the balls of her feet. Ready to sprint. Vega's breathing had steadied into the slow, controlled rhythm of someone preparing for violence.

Around us, wings spread. Claws extended. Tails coiled.

The Drakarn were built for this. Speed, strength, natural weapons. They could fly over obstacles I'd have to climb. Could smash through barriers I'd need to navigate around. Could cover ground in minutes that would take me an hour.

I couldn't compete with that.

So I wouldn't try.

The horn's blast split the air.

Chaos erupted.

Warriors launched in every direction. Wings beat, creating wind that nearly knocked me sideways. Claws scraped stone. Bodies collided as everyone fought for position, for the best routes, for any advantage they could seize.

I grabbed Lexa's arm and pulled her toward a smaller corridor at the square's edge. Not the main route. Not where the bulk of warriors were heading. Somewhere less obvious.

We hit the corridor at a dead run.

Behind us, the sounds of pursuit began. Roars. Wing beats. The thunder of dozens of warriors all trying to reach the same goal.

The Skalanth had started.

And I was either going to prove I belonged here or die trying.

9

TERRA

"YOU REALIZE this is going to be basically impossible without wings, right?" Vega's voice cut through the chaos of warriors launching themselves in every direction.

I pressed my back against the rough stone wall of a side corridor, watching scaled bodies blur past the opening. The sound of claws on rock was deafening. Wing beats created gusts that sent dust swirling. And then there were the roars of challenge and determination.

"I like being underestimated," I said.

Lexa appeared beside us, breathing hard from our sprint away from the main crush. "Being underestimated is great right up until someone underestimates you to death."

Fair point.

The corridor we'd ducked into was narrow enough that a Drakarn with spread wings couldn't follow easily. Perfect for humans, a tight squeeze for a Drakarn.

I leaned forward carefully, peering around the corner toward the main thoroughfare. Warriors streamed past, most heading upward toward the Temple district. Some flew. A few ran along the ground, relying on speed over altitude.

"We need a plan," Vega said. She'd pulled out a scrap of cloth and was wiping sweat from her face. Her gray eyes tracked movement beyond our hiding spot with the focus of someone cataloging threats. "Charging straight for the Temple is suicide. Half the senior warriors will be positioned along the main routes."

"I am aware of that." I shifted my weight, feeling the blade at my hip settle into a more comfortable position. "What are you thinking?"

"Tunnel routes." Vega pointed farther down the corridor. "I've scouted some of the lower passages. They're slower, but they're hidden. Less chance of running into warriors who can snap us like twigs."

"How much slower?" Lexa asked.

"Maybe double the time of a direct route. But we'd actually make it alive, so there's that."

I considered it.

The logic was sound.

Take the safe path, avoid confrontation, reach the Temple through routes the Drakarn wouldn't expect or bother watching. We might not win, but we'd survive. We'd complete the trial. We'd prove we could finish what we started.

But that wasn't why I was here.

"No," I said.

Vega's head snapped toward me. "No?"

"If we take the tunnels, we're just confirming what everyone already thinks. That humans can't compete directly. That we're too weak to handle the real challenge." I met her gaze. "I didn't enter this thing to hide in the shadows. I need to be *seen* doing this."

"You entered this thing to prove a point," Vega countered. "Dead people don't prove points. They just prove they were stupid."

"She's not wrong," Lexa said.

"I know she's not wrong." I pushed away from the wall, rolling my shoulders to loosen the tension building there. "But think about it. If we skulk through hidden passages and somehow manage to reach the blood-flame, what does that prove? That we're good at sneaking? Everyone already knows that. They've been calling us weak and fragile for months. Taking the coward's route just confirms it."

"The smart route," Vega corrected. "There's a difference between cowardice and tactics."

"Not in this."

Silence fell between us. Somewhere in the distance, metal rang against metal. A roar of pain or fury echoed off stone walls. The competition was already getting violent.

Lexa broke the quiet. "So what's the alternative? We run straight down the main street and hope nobody notices?"

"We be visible," I said, "but strategic. Not suicidal. We use the main routes enough that people see us. See us holding our own. But we're smart about when to engage and when to avoid." I looked at Vega. "You're the tactical genius. Tell me there's a way to make that work."

She stared at me for a long moment. Then she sighed, the sound carrying more resignation than agreement. "There might be. Emphasis on might."

"I'll take it."

"You're going to get us killed."

"People don't usually die in the Skalanth."

"That's not as comforting as you think it is," Lexa muttered.

Vega pulled out a small piece of charcoal she'd tucked into her belt and started sketching on the stone wall. A rough map took shape. Lines for corridors. Circles for major intersections. X marks for what I assumed were danger zones.

"Main routes are here, here, and here." She tapped three lines that converged toward the Temple district. "Most warriors will take the upper paths. Faster if you can fly. Senior warriors will be positioned at chokepoints." She marked several spots with heavy X's. "We avoid those. Stick to secondary routes that are still visible from the main thoroughfares. We'll be seen, but we won't be trapped."

"What about the Temple entrance?" I asked.

"That's where it gets messy." Vega's charcoal hovered over the map. "The Temple will be heavily guarded. No way around that. We'll have to either fight through or find another way in."

"We'll figure it out when we get there," I said. "First, we need to actually reach the Temple."

Vega nodded and wiped away her map with

one sleeve. "Stay close. Move fast. Don't engage unless we have to."

We moved back toward the main corridor, staying tight to the wall. The flow of warriors had thinned slightly as competitors spread throughout the city, but enough remained that stepping into the open felt like diving into rapids.

I went first.

The transition from shadow to light made me squint. The main thoroughfare was wider here, carved to accommodate Drakarn wings and tails. Spectators lined the upper levels, Scalvaris citizens who'd come to watch the Skalanth. Their voices created a droning background noise. Cheering. Commentary. Placing bets, probably.

Some of them noticed us immediately.

"Humans?"

"Is that the Warrior Lord's mate?"

"What are they doing here?"

The whispers spread like fire. I felt the weight of attention shift toward us. Hundreds of eyes. Judgment and curiosity and hostility all mixed together.

Keep moving. Don't react.

The street sloped upward, following the natural contours of the mountain. Ahead, I could see where it branched into multiple paths. Some leading deeper into the Temple district. Others curving toward different sections of the city.

I heard more whispers from the crowd.

"Give them ten minutes."

"I'm betting five."

"The Warrior Lord's going to lose his mind when his pet gets broken."

I kept walking. Let them talk. Words were just noise.

But the prickling sensation between my shoulder blades intensified. Being watched. Being judged. Every step documented and assessed.

"You okay?" Vega asked quietly.

"Fine."

"You don't look fine."

"I'm fine."

She didn't push. We turned onto a side street that ran parallel to the main route. Fewer spectators here, but still visible from the upper levels. Present but not suicidal.

The street narrowed as we climbed. Buildings carved from the mountain itself pressed close on either side. Some had windows that glowed with internal light. Others were dark, abandoned or used for storage. The architecture was beautiful in its way. Functional but decorated with carvings that depicted battles and ceremonies and moments from Scalvaris history.

I'd studied some of those carvings during my time here. Learned the stories. Tried to understand the culture I'd mated into.

None of those lessons had prepared me for this.

"Movement ahead," Lexa warned.

I looked up. A warrior descended from above, wings spread to control his fall. He landed maybe twenty meters in front of us, claws scraping stone. His scales were a mottled brown and gray, good camouflage against the rock. Young, probably mid-twenties. Confident in the way that came from never having been seriously challenged.

He saw us and grinned.

"Three little humans, all alone." He flexed his claws. "This is almost too easy."

"This doesn't have to be a fight," I said.

"You're funny." He took a step forward. "Capturing the Warrior Lord's mate during the Skalanth? That's a story I can tell for years."

I put my hand on the hilt of my blade. "That's not going to happen."

"I have wings. You have …" He made a show

of looking us over. "What do you have, exactly? Fragile skin? Breakable bones?"

Vega bristled. She didn't draw a weapon. Didn't make any obvious aggressive move. Just shifted her stance slightly, weight on the balls of her feet, hands loose at her sides.

The warrior noticed. His grin widened. "Oh, you want to fight? This should be entertaining."

Lexa circled to the warrior's left while I went right. Vega stayed center, drawing his attention. Classic triangle formation. Surround and overwhelm.

The warrior's confidence faltered slightly as he realized he was being flanked. His tail lashed. Wings flared partway, an instinctive threat display.

"Three on one?" He tried to sound contemptuous but didn't quite manage it. "Cowards."

She attacked.

Not with a blade. With her boot, sweeping low toward his ankle. He jumped back, wings beating once to gain altitude. Fast. But Lexa was already moving, grabbing a loose stone from the ground and hurling it at his head.

He twisted to avoid it, and I closed the distance. My blade came free of its sheath with a whisper of metal. I didn't try to stab. Just slashed at his extended wing membrane, forcing him to fold it or risk damage.

He folded.

And dropped.

Vega was there when he landed, driving her shoulder into his midsection. The impact sent him stumbling backward. His tail caught on a jutting piece of rock, and he went down hard, wings tangling beneath him.

I pressed my blade to his throat before he could recover.

"Yield," I said.

He stared up at me, shock written across his features. His chest heaved. Claws flexed uselessly against the stone.

"Yield," I repeated.

"You …" He seemed unable to finish the thought. "You're human."

"True." I didn't move the blade. "Yield or we keep going. Your choice."

He yielded.

I stepped back, sheathing my weapon. Vega and Lexa maintained their positions, ready in case he changed his mind. But the fight had gone out of him. He just lay there, staring at us like we'd violated some fundamental law of nature.

Maybe we had.

We left him there and continued up the street. None of us spoke until we'd put distance between us and the fallen warrior. Then Lexa started laughing. Quiet at first, then building until she had to stop walking and lean against a wall.

"Did you see his face?" She wiped tears from her eyes. "He couldn't believe it."

"Good." Vega's expression remained serious. "Maybe the next one think twice."

I had trouble believing that would happen.

The encounter had cost us time but bought us something more valuable. Proof that we could compete. That three humans working together could take down a Drakarn warrior. It wouldn't be enough to win the Skalanth, but it was a start.

The prickling sensation between my shoulders intensified.

I stopped walking and turned, scanning the rooftops and upper levels. Nothing obvious. Just the usual spectators watching from safe distances. But the feeling persisted. Someone was paying very close attention.

"What is it?" Vega asked.

"Someone's watching us."

"Kind of the point, remember?" Her tone was dry. "You wanted to be visible."

"This is different." I couldn't explain it. Just a gut feeling that had kept me alive through too many dangerous situations to ignore. "I think someone's tracking us."

Lexa followed my gaze upward. Her expression shifted from amused to alert. "I don't see anyone."

Who was it? Some minion from Karyseth? A warrior waiting to make his move?

We couldn't stop to worry.

We started moving again, faster now. Drakarn warriors passed us going the opposite direction, eliminated from competition and heading back toward the gathering square. Some had ash marks on their faces. Others just looked defeated.

The Temple district loomed ahead. I could see the massive entrance carved into the mountain's face. Pillars thick as ancient trees. Symbols etched deep into stone. Heat crystals the size of my head embedded in the archway, casting everything in shades of fire.

And warriors. So many warriors.

They clustered around the entrance like scales

on a dragon's hide. Senior warriors, judging by their size and the way they moved. Confident. Experienced. Ready to stop anyone who tried to pass.

"That's a lot of guards," Lexa observed.

"More than I expected," Vega agreed. She'd stopped at the edge of a market square that offered a clear view of the Temple. "We're not fighting through that."

"No," I said. "We're not."

Vega's face grew serious, and I could see thoughts whizzing by in her eyes. She pursed her lips and then nodded decisively.

She met my gaze steadily, no arguments. "Give me two minutes. When you see the guards move, run." She checked her weapons one more time. "Don't wait for me. Don't look back. Just get inside and finish this."

"Vega …"

She moved before either of us could say anything else. She slipped into the crowd of spectators that had gathered to watch the Temple entrance. Her auburn hair disappeared among the larger Drakarn bodies.

Two minutes.

I used the time to curse up and storm and then study the side passage she'd pointed to before running off like a big damn hero. It was there, barely visible between two carved pillars. Dark. Narrow. Probably designed for servants to move supplies without disrupting ceremonies.

Perfect for sneaking.

If we could reach it.

Lexa shifted beside me, her weight balanced and ready. "This is a terrible plan."

"I know."

"We're probably going to die."

"We're not going to die."

Movement at the Temple entrance. The guards shifted, attention drawn toward something in the market square. Voices rose. Not alarm yet, but curiosity.

Then Vega's voice cut through the noise, loud and challenging.

"Is this the best Scalvaris can offer? I've seen better guards at a freaking shopping mall!"

The effect was immediate. Warriors turned. Some laughed. Others bristled at the insult. Vega kept going, her voice carrying across the square.

"Come on! I'm one unarmed human! Surely someone here can catch me!"

She took off running.

The guards broke formation and gave chase.

And Lex and I had our way into the temple.

10

TERRA

THE TEMPLE CORRIDORS swallowed us up.

Stone pressed close on both sides, carved smooth centuries ago but still holding the city's heat like a living thing. My boots scraped against rock as Lexa and I pushed deeper into the passages, our breathing harsh in the confined space. Behind us, the sounds of Vega's distraction echoed and faded, replaced by the thunder of our own heartbeats.

I didn't let myself think about what was happening to her.

Couldn't.

The passage split ahead. Left or right, no obvious markers to indicate which led toward the sanctum. I chose left on instinct, trusting the upward slope to carry us closer to the Temple's heart.

Lexa followed without question, her knife already drawn. Blood ran down her forearm from a scratch she'd taken during our sprint past the Temple entrance. Not deep, but enough to leave a trail.

The corridor opened into a wider space, still narrow by Drakarn standards but enough for two people to stand side by side. Heat crystals embedded in the ceiling cast everything in dim light. The air tasted like smoke and old incense.

Movement ahead.

I threw up a hand, and Lexa froze. We pressed against the wall, making ourselves as small as possible. Footsteps approached, heavy and confident. Claws clicking on stone.

A green-scaled Drakarn warrior rounded the corner.

His wings were folded tight against his back to fit the space, and he carried a short blade that gleamed in the dim light. He saw us immediately.

His eyes widened. Then narrowed.

"Humans." He said it like a curse. "How did you get past the entrance?"

"We walked," I said.

His lip curled, showing fang. "Clever. It won't help you here."

He lunged.

The confined space worked against him. His wings scraped the walls as he tried to close the distance, slowing him just enough. I dropped low, blade coming up to meet his strike. Metal screamed against metal. The impact jarred up my arms, but I held firm, redirecting his momentum past me.

Lexa moved in from the side, her knife finding the gap between his scales at the back of his knee. Not deep enough to truly injure him, just enough to make him stumble.

He roared and spun, tail lashing. The appendage caught Lexa across the ribs and sent her crashing into the wall. She went down hard, breath exploding from her lungs.

I was already moving. I threw myself at his back, using his own height against him. My blade found the soft flesh of his wing and sliced through. Not a killing blow, but painful enough to make him forget about Lexa.

He twisted, trying to shake me off. I held on, wrapping my legs around his waist, one hand fisted in his hair. My other hand brought the blade up toward his throat.

"Yield," I hissed in his ear.

He bucked like a wild animal. My grip slipped. I went flying, hit the opposite wall, and tasted blood where I'd bitten my tongue.

Lexa was back on her feet. She threw herself at his legs, taking him down with sheer determination and no regard for her own safety. They fell together in a tangle of limbs and wings.

I scrambled up, ignoring the pain radiating through my shoulder where I'd hit stone. I crossed the distance in three strides and pressed my blade to the base of his skull.

"Back off," I repeated. "Or this gets worse."

He went still. His chest heaved. Fury radiated from him like heat from the crystals above.

"You fight like cowards," he spat.

"We fight to win." I didn't move the blade. "Is this over?"

He yielded.

We left him there, wings damaged, pride shattered. Lexa limped for the first few steps but forced herself into a steady pace. The cut on her arm was still bleeding. Her breathing sounded wrong, too shallow. Probably bruised ribs from that tail strike.

"You okay?" I asked.

"Fine."

She wasn't fine. Neither was I. My shoulder throbbed. My hands shook from adrenaline. The taste of blood in my mouth was a reminder of how close that fight had been.

But we were moving forward. That was what mattered.

The passage kept going. My calves burned. Sweat soaked through my shirt, mixing with the stone dust that coated everything. The heat intensified as we went on, pressing down like a physical weight.

Another intersection. This time, I chose right, following the sound of distant voices. Other participants, probably. The Skalanth was designed to force confrontation, to test warriors against each other as much as against the obstacles themselves.

We were walking into a meat grinder.

The voices grew louder. Multiple speakers, arguing or fighting or both. The passage opened into a chamber carved from solid rock, maybe twenty meters across. Heat crystals the size of my fist lined the walls.

Six Drakarn warriors filled the space.

They'd been fighting each other, that much was obvious. Scales were scratched. Wings torn. One warrior sat against the wall, ash mark already visible on his shoulder. Eliminated.

They all turned when we entered.

Silence fell like a blade.

Then chaos.

Two of them came at us immediately, seeing easy targets. The others went back to fighting each other, too focused on their own competition to care about humans. The chamber became a mess of bodies and violence, everyone trying to reach the exit on the far side that led deeper into the Temple.

I ducked under a wing strike, felt claws rake across my back. Fabric tore but didn't reach skin. Lexa was beside me, her knife flashing as she drove it toward a warrior's exposed flank. He twisted away, but the movement opened him up to another participant's attack.

We used the chaos. Stayed low. Moved fast. Let the Drakarn fight each other while we navigated the edges of the battle.

A massive warrior with brown scales blocked our path to the exit. He wasn't fighting anyone, just standing guard, waiting. Smart. Let the others exhaust themselves while he stayed fresh.

His eyes found mine. Recognition flickered across his features.

"The Warrior Lord's pet." His voice carried over the sounds of combat. "This will be a story."

"Get out of the way," I said.

"Make me."

Lexa threw her knife.

It wasn't meant to hit him. Just to distract. He batted it aside with one clawed hand, and in that moment of diverted attention, I ran straight at him.

But not to fight.

I dropped into a baseball slide, using the smooth stone floor and my own momentum to carry me between his legs. He grabbed for me but missed, his claws closing on empty air.

I came up on the other side and kept running.

Lexa followed, scooping up her knife as she passed. The brown-scaled warrior roared behind us, but he was too slow. We hit the exit corridor at full speed and didn't look back.

The passage beyond was narrow again. Single

file. My lungs burned. My legs felt like they were made of lead. But I pushed harder, driven by fear and determination in equal measure.

Vega had sacrificed herself for this. I couldn't waste it.

The thought of her facing guards alone, getting captured, marked with ash and sent home in disgrace, it sat in my chest like a stone. She'd done it willingly. She'd be fine tomorrow. But that didn't make the guilt any lighter.

"Stop it," Lexa said from behind me.

"What?"

"Whatever you're thinking. Stop it." Her voice was sharp. "Vega made her choice. You don't get to feel bad about it. That's an insult to her decision."

The words hit harder than any punch could have.

She was right. Vega had chosen this path knowing exactly what it meant. Treating her sacrifice like something to feel shameful about diminished the strength it took to make that choice.

"Okay," I said.

"Okay?"

"You're right. Guilt is for later." I forced

myself to focus on the passage ahead. "After we finish this."

"With an attitude like that, you're lucky a therapist didn't crash down on this heap with us."

I snorted.

The corridor opened into another chamber, this one vertical. A shaft that climbed upward into darkness, but wall that wasn't completely smooth, there were natural handholds at human-spaced intervals. It was the kind of climb that would be trivial for a Drakarn with wings. For us, it was a death trap.

I looked up, trying to gauge the distance. Maybe fifteen meters.

"We can't climb that," Lexa said.

"We have to."

"Terra …"

"Do you see another way up?" I circled the chamber, running my hands along the walls. Looking for anything. Like for a hidden passage to appear out of nowhere.

Nothing.

Just stone and the mocking shaft above.

Voices echoed from the passage we'd just left. More warriors, heading this way. We were about to be trapped in a dead end with nowhere to go but up.

"I'll boost you," Lexa said. "Get you started."

"That's not going to work."

"It has to work. We don't have another option." She moved to the wall, lacing her fingers together to form a step. "Come on. We're wasting time."

She was right. Again.

I put my boot in her hands, and she lifted, grunting with effort. I grabbed the lowest handhold, pulled myself up. My shoulder screamed in protest. The muscles in my arms shook.

I reached for the next hold. Pulled. Reached. Pulled.

Below me, Lexa jumped for the lowest handhold. Her fingers caught. Held. She started climbing, her face set in grim determination.

The voices behind us grew louder. Warriors entering the chamber. Seeing us on the wall.

"Climbing?" Someone laughed. "This I have to see."

I didn't look down. Just kept moving. Hand over hand. The holds were rough against my palms, volcanic stone that wanted to shred skin.

My arms burned. My shoulder felt like it was tearing itself apart.

Halfway up.

Lexa was maybe three meters below me, climbing with single-minded focus. Her injured arm left blood smears on the stone.

Something hit the wall beside my head.

I jerked back instinctively, nearly lost my grip. Looked down and saw a Drakarn warrior at the base of the shaft, another stone in his hand. He was using us for target practice.

"Keep going," Lexa shouted.

Another stone flew past. This one clipped my leg, sent pain radiating through my calf. I gritted my teeth and reached for the next hold.

The top of the shaft appeared above me. A ledge. Safety.

I pulled myself over the edge and collapsed, chest heaving. Every muscle in my body shook. But I was up.

Lexa's hand appeared at the ledge. I grabbed it, hauled her up with strength I didn't know I still had. She rolled onto solid ground beside me, gasping.

Below, wings beat. The warriors were flying

up the shaft, taking seconds to cover the distance we'd spent minutes climbing.

"Move," I said.

We ran.

The passage here was wider, carved with more care. Symbols decorated the walls, religious markings I didn't have time to decipher. The air grew thicker with incense. We were close to the sanctum. Had to be.

The corridor opened into a final chamber.

Larger than the others. Circular. Heat crystals embedded in a pattern that made the whole space glow like the inside of a forge. And at the far end, through an archway carved with protective sigils, I could see it.

The blood-flame.

It sat on a pedestal in the center of what had to be the inner sanctum. Pulsing with internal light. Red and gold and alive. So close I could almost feel its heat from here.

But between us and that archway stood at least a dozen Drakarn warriors.

Not guards. Warriors in the Skalanth. All of them converging on the same goal. All of them willing to go through anyone who got in their way.

The chamber erupted into violence. Warriors fighting each other, fighting us, fighting anyone who got close to that archway. I lost track of Lexa almost immediately, caught up in the chaos of bodies and wings and claws.

A tail swept my legs. I went down, rolled, came up with my blade already moving. Caught a warrior across the arm, not deep but enough to make him back off.

Someone grabbed my hair from behind. Yanked hard enough to bring tears to my eyes. I twisted, drove my elbow backward into scales. The grip released.

The archway was maybe ten meters away. It might as well have been a thousand.

I fought toward it anyway. One step. Two. Using every dirty trick I'd learned in eight months of survival. Nothing honorable. Nothing fair. Just desperation and the will to keep moving forward.

A massive shape blocked my path. Purple scales. Yellow eyes.

The novice who'd cornered me in the corridor days ago.

Recognition flared in his expression. Then something uglier. Vindication.

"Say goodnight, human."

He raised his clawed hand, ready to strike.

Lexa's scream cut through the chaos. "*Terra!*"

I turned, saw her fighting off two warriors at once, saw the purple-scaled bastard's claws descending toward my head.

Then something gray and fast dropped from above.

Nyx landed between us, steel-gray scales gleaming in the crystal light. His wings spread wide, blocking the purple warrior from reaching me.

He intercepted the strike with brutal efficiency, his own claws catching the purple warrior's wrist and twisting. Bone cracked. The warrior screamed and fell back.

My heart stopped.

We were caught. It was over. A senior warrior had found us, and there was no way Lexa and I could fight our way past him.

Lexa appeared at my side, putting herself between me and Nyx. Her knife was out, held in a grip that shook with exhaustion but didn't waver.

"Run," she said. "I'll hold him off."

"Lexa, no …"

"Run!" She shoved me toward the archway. "Don't waste this. Go!"

Lexa lunged at him, and he moved to counter. They became a tangle of motion that blocked the other warriors from reaching me.

I ran.

Guilt tore at me with every step.

Vega had sacrificed herself. Lexa was sacrificing herself. I couldn't let those choices mean nothing.

The archway loomed ahead. The sanctum beyond it was empty. No guards. No participants. Just the blood-flame on its pedestal, pulsing like a heartbeat.

My boots hit the sanctum floor. The chamber was smaller than I'd expected, intimate. Carved with reverence. The blood-flame's light filled every corner, warm and alive.

I could see it clearly now. Multifaceted. Beautiful. The goal of the Skalanth. The symbol of everything I was trying to prove.

Victory was three meters away.

I ran toward it.

And stopped.

Darrokar stood between me and the blood-flame.

"*Luvae.*"

11

DARROKAR

THE BLOOD-FLAME PULSED behind me like a second heartbeat.

I'd stood guard in this sanctum for three hours, watching novice after novice attempt to breach the inner chamber. Most never made it past the outer defenses. Those who did faced Rath's blade or my claws and fell back, marked with ash, dreams of glory extinguished.

It was duty. Sacred and necessary. The kind of responsibility that came with my position as Warrior Lord.

But right now, duty felt like chains.

Terra stood in the archway, chest heaving, covered in blood and stone dust and the evidence of every fight she'd survived to reach this place.

Her green eyes locked on mine, and the mate-bond ignited between us with enough force to steal my breath.

Pain. Exhaustion. Determination so fierce it burned.

All of it flooded through the connection we shared, mixing with my own horror and pride until I couldn't separate what I felt from what she felt.

She'd actually done it.

Made it through the traps, the obstacles, the warriors who'd tried to stop her. Fought her way to the inner sanctum using nothing but human stubbornness and the skills I'd taught her myself.

Part of me wanted to roar with pride. Wanted to gather her against my chest and tell her how magnificent she was, how strong, how absolutely insane for attempting this in the first place.

The other part wanted to lock her in our quarters and never let her risk herself like this again.

Neither option was available.

I was the final guardian. She was a competitor. And the blood-flame sat beyond us like the ultimate test.

"Luvae." The word came out rougher than I'd intended.

She didn't respond. Just stared at me with those eyes that had haunted me since the moment I'd first scented her. Blood trickled from a cut above her eyebrow. Her shirt was torn, exposing scratches across her ribs. She favored her left leg, putting more weight on the right.

Injured. Exhausted. Barely standing.

And still looking at me like she had any chance of getting past.

My claws flexed. The sanctum suddenly felt too small, the air too thick. Every instinct I possessed screamed conflicting commands.

Protect her.

Stop her.

Let her pass.

I was Warrior Lord. I had duties. Responsibilities that extended beyond my personal desires.

But I was also her mate. And watching her bleed, watching her struggle to stay upright, it carved something out of my chest that had nothing to do with duty or honor or sacred tradition.

"There is no shame in failing now," I said, keeping my voice level. "You've proven yourself.

Made it farther than anyone expected. You can yield with honor."

Her laugh was sharp enough to draw blood. "Can I?"

"Yes."

"And what happens then?" She took a step forward, limping but steady. "I walk out of here with my head held high, knowing I gave it my best effort? Everyone pats me on the back and says how brave I was for trying?"

"Something like that."

"Bullshit." Another step. "You know exactly what happens. I become the human who couldn't finish. Who needed special consideration. Who proved that my kind doesn't belong." Her jaw tightened. "I didn't come this far to quit three meters from the goal."

"You came this far to prove a point. You've done that."

"Not yet, I haven't."

She moved again, angling toward my left side. Testing. Looking for an opening that didn't exist.

I shifted to block her path, wings spreading slightly to fill the space. "Don't make me stop you."

"Then don't stand in my way."

"I'm the final guardian, Terra. This is my duty."

"I know." Her hand dropped to the blade at her hip. "Which is why I'm not asking you to step aside."

The sight of her drawing that weapon, the one I'd helped her choose, the one we'd trained with together, it did something complicated to my insides.

She was going to fight me.

Actually fight me, here in the sacred sanctum, with the blood-flame as witness and the weight of tradition pressing down on both of us.

I should have felt outrage. Offense at the challenge. This was my role, my responsibility, and she was forcing me to fulfill it in the worst possible way.

Instead, I felt something closer to anticipation.

"Last chance," I said. "Yield now and walk out with dignity."

She snorted. "Make me."

Then she attacked.

Not recklessly. Not with the wild desperation of someone who had nothing to lose. She came at me with technique, with strategy, using footwork

I'd drilled into her during countless sparring sessions.

I parried her first strike, redirecting the blade rather than meeting it head-on. The screech of metal on claw echoed off the sanctum walls. She flowed with the deflection, already moving into her next attack before I'd fully reset my stance.

She'd gotten faster since we'd started training together.

Her blade swept low, aiming for my knee. I lifted my leg, letting the strike pass beneath, and countered with my tail. She jumped it, barely, and used the momentum to spin away before I could grab her.

We circled each other in the confined space. The dim red light painted her in shades of fire and shadow. Sweat cut tracks through the dust on her face. Her breathing came hard but controlled, measured in a way that spoke of discipline rather than panic.

She'd learned. Adapted. Taken everything I'd taught her and made it her own.

Pride swelled in my chest, fierce and unwanted.

"You've improved," I said.

"I had a good teacher." She feinted right, then went left. The blade came up toward my ribs.

I caught her wrist before the strike could land, my claws gentle despite the combat. Held her there, close enough to see the gold flecks in her green eyes. Close enough to smell blood and sweat and the underlying scent that marked her as mine.

"This doesn't have to happen," I said quietly.

"Yes, it does." She twisted in my grip, using a joint lock I'd shown her just last week. The move should have broken my hold.

Would have, if I'd been anyone else.

I was twice her size with natural advantages she'd never possess. Strength. Reach. Scales that turned aside blades that would cut human flesh to ribbons.

But I didn't use those advantages. Didn't crush her wrist or throw her across the chamber or end this with the kind of overwhelming force that would leave her unconscious on the sanctum floor.

Instead, I released her and stepped back.

She came at me again immediately.

The fight became a dance. Her attacking, me defending, both of us moving through patterns we'd practiced until they were muscle memory.

She knew how I'd respond to each strike. I knew how she'd flow from one technique to the next.

I put my whole focus into the fight. A hundred warriors could have run past us, and I wouldn't have noticed.

It should have made the combat predictable. Boring.

It didn't.

Because this wasn't training. This was real. Stakes that went beyond bruised pride or lessons learned. She was fighting for something that mattered to her in ways I was only beginning to understand.

And I was fighting to stop her from getting hurt.

Her blade found the gap between my scales at my shoulder, not deep enough to cause real damage but enough to sting. I hissed and grabbed for her, but she was already moving, already flowing into her next attack.

She'd studied me. Learned my patterns the same way I'd learned hers. Every weakness I'd shown during our sparring sessions, every tell that preceded my strikes, she'd cataloged and memorized.

My clever, brilliant, absolutely infuriating mate.

I caught her blade between my claws and twisted, trying to disarm her. She let the weapon go rather than fight for it, dropping into a crouch and sweeping my legs with her own.

I went down, more from surprise than actual force, and she was on me before I could recover. Straddling my chest, hands pressed against my shoulders, pinning me with her weight.

Which was laughable. She weighed maybe a third of what I did. I could throw her off without effort.

But I didn't.

I lay there, looking up at her, watching her chest heave with exertion. Blood from the cut above her eyebrow dripped onto my scales. Her hair had come loose from its tie and fell around her face in a wild tangle.

She was beautiful.

Fierce and determined and so completely out of her depth that it made my chest ache.

"Yield," she said.

I laughed. Couldn't help it. The sound erupted from me, genuine and surprised. "You're demanding I yield?"

"Why not? I've got you pinned."

"Luvae, I could remove you from this position in three different ways without even trying."

"But you won't." Her eyes held mine. "Because you don't want to hurt me."

She was right. And she knew it. Was using my own protective instincts against me.

I reached up slowly, giving her time to react, and cupped her face in my palm. My claws were careful against her soft skin. "This doesn't change anything. You still can't reach the blood-flame."

"Can't I?" She leaned into my touch, just slightly. Just enough to make my breath catch. "You're not exactly stopping me right now."

"I'm being gentle."

"I know." Something shifted in her expression. Softened. "You're always gentle with me. Even when you shouldn't be."

She was right. I pulled my strikes, redirected instead of crushing, treated her like she was made of glass even when she'd proven again and again that she was stronger than that.

Because I couldn't bear the thought of breaking her.

But in doing so, I'd given her an advantage. Made her believe she could actually win this confrontation through strategy and determination alone.

I sat up, taking her with me. She didn't resist, just adjusted her position until she was sitting in my lap, legs wrapped around my waist. The intimacy of it was jarring given the circumstances.

"You need to yield," I said.

"We both know I'm not going to do that, baby."

This was insane. We were fighting in a sacred chamber, surrounded by the weight of tradition and duty, and she was calling me baby like we were alone in our quarters.

I loved her so much it physically hurt.

"Terra." I tried to inject authority into my voice. Failed. "This has to end."

"Then let me pass."

"I can't."

"Can't or won't?"

"Both." I stood, lifting her with me, and set her gently on her feet. "I'm the final guardian. If I let you pass without a real fight, I undermine the entire trial."

"So we keep fighting." She retrieved her blade from where it had fallen. "Until one of us yields or I find a way past you."

"There is no way past me."

"There's always a way." She settled back into a ready stance. "I just have to find it."

The determination in her voice made something twist in my chest. She actually believed she could win this. Believed that human stubbornness and tactical thinking could overcome the fundamental reality of our physical differences.

It would have been endearing if it wasn't so dangerous.

I spread my wings fully, blocking any path to the blood-flame. "I don't want to hurt you."

"Then this should be easy." She scooped up her blade from where it had fallen and attacked again.

This time, I didn't hold back quite as much. Met her strikes with real force, used my tail to sweep her legs, my wings to create wind that threw off her balance. I was still careful, still pulling the truly dangerous moves, but I stopped treating her like she'd shatter at the first real contact.

She adapted immediately. Used my size against me, staying close where my wings were less effective. Targeted joints and gaps in my scales with precision that spoke of serious study. Made me work for every defensive position.

The fight intensified. Faster. Harder. Both of us pushing in ways we never had during practice.

And despite everything, despite the duty and the tradition and the impossible situation we'd found ourselves in, I was enjoying this.

Actually enjoying combat for the first time in years.

Not because of the violence or the test of skill. Because of her. Because fighting Terra meant being fully present, fully engaged, matching wits and strength with someone who refused to make it easy.

She made me better. Sharper. More alive.

Even when she was actively trying to get past me to steal a sacred gem.

I caught her in a grapple, arms wrapped around her waist, lifting her off the ground. She immediately went for a pressure point at my neck, fingers finding the spot with unerring accuracy. Pain radiated down my spine, sharp enough to make my grip loosen.

She dropped, rolled, came up running.

I was faster. Caught her around the waist again, this time prepared for her counterattack.

Held her suspended in the air, her legs kicking uselessly.

"Yield!" I demanded.

"No!"

"Terra, this is ridiculous. You can't win."

"Watch me!"

She twisted in my grip with enough violence that I had to adjust my hold or risk actually hurting her. The moment my arms shifted, she drove her elbow backward into my ribs. Hard enough to make me grunt.

I set her down and immediately regretted it.

She spun, blade coming up in an arc that would have opened my throat if I hadn't jerked back. The tip of her weapon scraped across my jaw, drawing a thin line of blood.

We both froze.

"Darrokar …"

The sound of combat erupted from the corridor beyond the sanctum.

We both turned toward the archway. Voices raised in challenge. The clash of weapons. Wings beating against stone.

More participants, fighting their way toward the inner chamber.

Terra's attention snapped back to me. I saw

the calculation in her eyes. Saw her recognize that my focus had split, that I'd have to divide my attention between her and whatever was coming through that archway.

Three Drakarn warriors burst into the sanctum.

Young. Aggressive. Their scales were scratched from previous fights, their weapons already drawn. They saw me and hesitated for just a moment.

Rath could probably handle them. I could pursue Terra and end her foolishness.

Instead, I turned from her and went to meet the young warriors claw to claw.

12

TERRA

THE SANCTUM WAS EMPTY.

I stood, chest heaving, blood dripping from the cut above my eyebrow, and stared at the bare pedestal where the blood-flame should have been.

Gone.

Someone had slipped past while I'd been fighting Darrokar. While I'd been so focused on proving I could match him blow for blow, another warrior had grabbed the prize and disappeared into the tunnels beyond.

I wanted to scream. Wanted to collapse right there on the stone floor and let exhaustion take me. My shoulder throbbed where I'd slammed into a wall three chambers back. My ribs ached from a tail strike I hadn't dodged fast enough.

Every muscle in my body felt like it had been wrung out and left to dry.

But I didn't collapse.

Because giving up now, after everything, would make this whole insane venture meaningless.

I limped across the sanctum, my boots scraping against stone that had been polished smooth by centuries of ceremony. The pedestal stood in the center of the chamber, carved from volcanic rock and inlaid with symbols I'd hadn't yet learned to read. Empty. Mocking.

Whoever had taken the blood-flame couldn't have much of a lead. Minutes, maybe. The finish line was at the city's edge, a solid distance even for a Drakarn with wings. If I moved fast, if I pushed through the pain and exhaustion, I might still intercept them.

Might.

The word tasted bitter.

I'd fought so hard to get here. Survived obstacles designed to break warriors twice my size. Taken down Drakarn competitors through sheer stubbornness and tactics I'd learned from watching Darrokar drill his warriors. Made it all the way to the inner sanctum only to arrive seconds too late.

The unfairness of it burned in my chest.

But standing here dwelling on it wouldn't change anything. I needed to move. Now.

I turned toward the exit corridor. My legs protested the first step. The second was worse. By the third, I'd found a rhythm that was more hobble than run but at least kept me moving forward.

The tunnel beyond the sanctum was narrow and dark, lit by heat crystals spaced far enough apart that shadows pooled between them. My breathing echoed off the walls, harsh and ragged. The sound reminded me just how alone I was down here.

No Vega creating distractions. No Lexa watching my back. Just me and the growing certainty that I'd failed.

I pushed the thought away and kept running.

The passage sloped downward. My boots slipped on smooth stone worn by generations of temple servants. I caught myself on the wall, felt rough volcanic rock scrape against my palm. The pain was sharp and immediate and somehow grounding.

I was still here. Still moving. Still in this.

Voices echoed from somewhere ahead. I couldn't make out words, just the rumble of Drakarn conversation bouncing through the tunnels. Other warriors, probably.

I rounded a corner and nearly collided with a group of three warriors heading the opposite direction. Ash marks stained their shoulders, dark against their scales. Eliminated. They saw me and stopped, blocking the passage.

The one in front had rust-colored scales and a fresh cut across his snout. His eyes narrowed when he recognized me.

"The Warrior Lord's human." He said it like an accusation.

I didn't have time for this. "Let me pass."

"You're going the wrong way." He didn't move. "Eliminated warriors return to the gathering square."

"I'm not eliminated."

"You should be." His tail lashed behind him, the tip scraping against stone.

The other two shifted, flanking him. Not aggressive yet but getting there. My hand dropped to my blade's hilt, fingers closing around leather that was slick with my own sweat.

"I don't want trouble," I said.

"Neither did we. But here you are, making a mockery of our traditions."

Something hot and furious flared in my chest. I was exhausted. Injured. Running on fumes and desperation. And this asshole wanted to lecture me about tradition while blocking my path.

"Get out of my way," I said.

He laughed. The sound was harsh and ugly. "Or what? You'll fight all three of us?"

I would if I had to. The thought was insane. Three on one, when I could barely stand. But I'd come too far to let some bitter warrior stop me now.

I drew my blade.

The rust-scaled warrior's expression shifted. Surprise, then something darker. He reached for his own weapon. And then his silent friend placed his claws on his arm.

"We are honor bound to stop fighting," he reminded rust-scales.

Rust-scales cursed.

I ran, taking full advantage of the hesitation.

My body was screaming now. The adrenaline that had carried me through the fights was gone, leaving nothing but pain and exhaustion. My shoulder felt like someone had driven a spike through it. The cut above my eyebrow kept bleeding, sending warm trickles down the side of my face. My ribs protested every breath.

But I kept moving.

The tunnel opened into a wider passage, one that I now recognized. This route would take me past the lower markets and eventually to the city's eastern edge where the finish line waited. I was close now. Minutes away.

Not that it mattered. Even if I sprouted wings and flew, I was too far behind.

But I could finish. Could cross that line and prove I'd completed the trial even if I hadn't won it.

The passage climbed, forcing me to use my hands as much as my feet. The stone was rough here, unpolished, meant for utility rather than beauty. My palms scraped against it, adding new injuries to the collection I'd accumulated.

I hauled myself up the final incline.

The finish line stood maybe a hundred meters away. A raised platform where priests in ceremonial robes waited. A crowd had gathered around it, spectators and eliminated warriors all pressing close to see the conclusion of the Skalanth.

And standing on that platform, holding the blood-flame high above his head, was a warrior I didn't recognize. His scales were a deep red, his wings spread in a victory display that made him look twice his actual size.

A priest sounded the horn.

The blast rolled across the city, deep and resonant, announcing the Skalanth's end. The winner had been declared. The trial was over.

I'd failed.

The knowledge settled in my chest, heavy and cold. I'd fought so hard. Survived so much. Made it farther than anyone expected a human to go. And it hadn't been enough.

Disappointment threatened to pull me under. I stood there in the fading light, covered in blood and dust and failure, and felt the weight of every choice that had brought me here.

Then I saw Vega.

She stood at the edge of the crowd, ash covering her face, and her expression was pure defiance. Zarvash loomed beside her, his face twisted in what looked like fury and relief in equal measure. But Vega wasn't looking at him. She was looking at me.

Our eyes met across the distance. She raised her chin slightly. A challenge. A question.

Are you going to slink away or stand tall?

I knew my answer.

I started walking toward the platform. My limp was worse now, my body finally acknowledging all the damage I'd done to it. But I kept my head up, my shoulders back. Let the crowd see me approaching as more warriors began to journey back from the Temple.

Whispers rippled through the assembled warriors. I felt their eyes tracking my progress. Some hostile. Some curious. A few that might have been impressed.

The red-scaled winner noticed me. His victory display faltered slightly as he watched me climb the steps to the platform. The priests turned, their expressions ranging from surprise to disapproval.

I didn't care.

I reached the top and stood beside the winner and the other gathered warriors who hadn't been eliminated, looking out at the crowd. At the warriors who'd competed and lost. At the spectators who'd come to watch. At the city that had tested me and found me wanting.

The red-scaled winner looked at me, his

expression complicated. Then he did something I didn't expect.

He inclined his head slightly. Acknowledgment, warrior to warrior.

I returned the gesture.

A procession formed. The winner led, bloodflame held high. Behind him came the other warriors who'd reached the sanctum and survived. Maybe a dozen of us total, out of the hundreds who'd started.

I took my place near the back, falling in beside a warrior with dark green scales whose wing was hanging limply. He glanced at me, then forward again, but didn't protest my presence.

We marched through Scalvaris's streets. The route took us past the main thoroughfares, through market squares, along the river's edge. Spectators lined the path, cheering or silent depending on their opinions.

I saw humans in the crowd. Selene and Orla and Kaiya, their faces bright with something that looked like pride. Kinsley with tears streaming down her cheeks. Reika standing close to Omvar, her expression cautiously hopeful.

No Lexa.

The absence twisted in my gut. Where was she? Had she been injured? Worse? The questions circled in my head, feeding worry I couldn't afford right now. I'd find her later, find out what happened.

The procession continued. My legs threatened to give out with every step, but I locked my knees and kept moving. Let the pain fuel me instead of stopping me.

We reached the feast hall. The massive chamber was carved into the mountain's heart, its ceiling supported by pillars thick as ancient trees. Heat crystals embedded in the walls cast everything in warm light. Tables stretched the length of the space, already laden with food and drink.

The Blade Council sat at the head table. Darrokar in the center, flanked by his warriors. Rath on his right, Khorlar on his left. Zarvash glowering at the spot where Vega would sit. Vyne looking oddly pleased despite everything.

I walked into that hall with my head high. Let them see me limping. Let them see the blood and the exhaustion and the evidence of every fight I'd survived. I'd earned this. Earned my place among the warriors who'd completed the trial.

The grumbling I'd expected didn't come. A few warriors shot hostile looks my way, but most were too focused on the feast ahead to care about one human's presence.

I made my way to the head table and took the seat beside Darrokar. He didn't speak immediately, just looked at me with an expression that held too many emotions to name. Fury that I'd risked myself. Relief that I'd survived. Pride that I'd made it this far.

I met his gaze steadily. Waited for the lecture. The recriminations. The anger I knew he had every right to feel.

Instead, he reached under the table and took my hand. His claws were gentle against my scraped palm, his scales warm where they pressed against my skin.

"You're insane," he said quietly.

"I know."

"You could have died."

"I didn't."

"You didn't win."

I felt my mouth curve into something that wasn't quite a smile. Looked at the assembled warriors, at the feast laid out before us, at the city that had tested me and the mate who'd tried to stop me.

"Next year," I said, loud enough for the nearby warriors to hear, "I'm going to win."

Darrokar's hand tightened on mine. His expression shifted from complicated emotions to something simpler. Clearer.

"You're going to be the death of me, *luvae*," he said.

"Probably."

Around us, the feast began. Warriors filled their plates and raised their cups. Conversations started, arguments broke out, laughter echoed off stone walls. The Skalanth was over, and life in Scalvaris continued.

I sat beside my mate, surrounded by warriors who'd tried to break me, in a city that still wasn't sure I belonged. My body ached. My pride was bruised.

But I'd finished. I'd survived. And I'd set my sights on next year's victory with the same stubborn determination that had carried me this far.

Let them doubt me. Let them whisper that humans didn't belong in Drakarn trials. Let Karyseth and her followers plot and scheme and try to use my failure as ammunition.

I'd be back. Stronger. Faster. Better prepared.

And next time, I wouldn't just reach the sanctum.

I'd win.

13

TERRA

THE WATER WAS ALMOST TOO hot.

Steam rose from the surface of the bathing pool in lazy spirals, catching the light and turning everything hazy. I sat on the submerged stone bench, water lapping at my collarbones, and watched Darrokar through the mist.

He hadn't said much since we'd returned to our quarters. Just stripped off his ceremonial armor with methodical precision, checked me over for injuries with hands that were gentle but thorough, and guided me toward the pool with a look that suggested he had thoughts.

Many thoughts. None of them simple.

Now he sat across from me, wings spread slightly to either side. The light painted his obsidian scales in shades of fire, making him look like something carved from volcanic glass and brought to life. The ring I'd given him rested on his index finger, a sign of everything there was between us. He had to be pissed at me, but even now, he wore the ring. His golden eyes tracked my every movement, and I could see emotions in his expression that I couldn't quite separate.

Pride. Frustration. Relief. Desire.

All of it tangled together until I couldn't tell where his feelings ended and mine began.

I flexed my fingers under the water, watching the way the ripples distorted the view of my hands. My knuckles were scraped. My palms were raw. The cut above my eyebrow had stopped bleeding but would probably leave a scar. Small prices for what I'd accomplished.

Or tried to.

"So," I finally said. "On a scale of one to ten, how angry are you?"

Darrokar's tail moved beneath the water, the tip breaking the surface for just a moment before disappearing again. "That depends on the scale."

"Human scale. One being mildly annoyed, ten being ready to lock me in our quarters for the next decade."

"Fifteen."

I laughed despite myself. The sound echoed off the stone walls, too loud in the quiet space. "That's not how it works."

"You asked how angry I was. I answered." His voice was calm. The kind of calm that came from very carefully controlling what you actually wanted to say. "You entered a sacred trial designed to test Drakarn warriors. You fought your way through obstacles that could have killed you. You made it to the inner sanctum and then tried to fight me for access to the blood-flame."

"Technically, I got past you."

"Terra."

The way he said my name made something clench in my chest. Not quite a warning, not quite a plea. Just my name, weighted with everything he wasn't saying.

I shifted on the bench, water sloshing around me. "I know I crossed some lines."

"Some lines." He repeated the words like he was tasting them. "You crossed every line. You risked yourself in ways that made me question whether you have any sense of self-preservation. You forced me to choose between my duty as Warrior Lord and my need to keep you safe."

Each point landed like a stone. I felt them settle in my gut, heavy and uncomfortable. He wasn't wrong. About any of it.

"I'm sorry," I said quietly.

"Are you?"

The question caught me off guard. I looked up, met his gaze across the steaming water. "Yes. I'm sorry I put you in that position. Sorry I made you worry. Sorry I dragged Vega and Lexa into my mess."

"But you're not sorry you entered the Skalanth."

It wasn't a question. He already knew the answer.

"No," I admitted. "I'm not sorry about that."

Something shifted in his expression. The careful control cracked just slightly, letting me see the turmoil underneath. "Why?"

"Because I needed to know if I could do it. Needed to prove to myself that I could compete in your world on your terms." I moved through the water toward him, slowly, giving him time to stop me if he wanted. "I know it was reckless. I know it was dangerous. But I can't spend the rest of my life wondering if I'm only here because of who I'm mated to instead of who I am."

"You're here because you're strong. Capable. Brilliant." His tail found my leg under the water, wrapping around my calf with gentle pressure. "You don't need to risk your life in trials to prove that."

"Maybe not to you." I reached him, close enough to see the gold flecks in his eyes. "But I needed to prove it to myself."

He studied my face for a long moment. Then his hand came up, cupping my jaw with claws that were careful against my skin. "You're going to give me gray scales."

"You keep saying that. I still don't see any gray."

"Give it time." His thumb stroked across my cheekbone, the pad rough against my flushed skin. "You terrified me today, luvae."

The admission hit harder than any anger could have. I leaned into his touch, letting the warmth of his palm seep into me. "I know. I'm sorry."

"Stop apologizing with words."

I blinked. "What?"

"You keep saying you're sorry. Prove it." His eyes darkened, the gold taking on a deeper hue.

"Show me you understand what you put me through."

The challenge hung between us, electric and weighted. He wanted me to make amends like a Drakarn. With action.

I could work with that.

I moved closer, straddling his lap in one smooth motion. The water displaced around us, sloshing against the pool's edges. His hands came to my hips automatically, steadying me, and I felt the flex of his claws against my skin.

"Like this?" I asked, my voice dropping lower.

His breath hitched. Just slightly, but I caught it. "That's a start."

I kissed him.

Not gentle. Not apologetic. I kissed him with all the pent-up emotion from the day, all the fear and triumph and desperate need to prove I was still there, still his, still alive despite everything. His mouth opened under mine, and I tasted heat and want and something darker that made my pulse spike.

His claws pricked against my hips. He pulled me closer until there was no space between us, just water and skin and scales and the building pressure of the mate-bond flaring hot in my chest.

I broke the kiss to trail my lips along his jaw, feeling the slight roughness where I'd cut him during our fight. The wound had already healed, but I kissed it anyway. An apology for drawing his blood. An acknowledgment of how far I'd pushed.

He made a sound low in his throat, somewhere between a growl and a groan. The vibration of it traveled through his chest into mine, making me shiver despite the heat of the water.

"Terra." My name again, but different this time. Rougher. Needier.

"I'm here." I kissed down his neck, finding the spot where his pulse beat strong beneath his scales. "I'm safe. I'm yours."

His tail tightened around my leg, the tip sliding higher up my thigh. The sensation made me gasp against his skin.

He knew exactly what he was doing, knew every spot that made me melt.

Two could play that game.

I let my hands wander, tracing the hard planes of his chest, feeling the way his muscles jumped under my touch. Down his sides, careful of his wings where they spread in the water. Lower, until I found what I was looking for.

His cock was already hard, the tip just

breaking the surface of the water. I wrapped my hand around it, feeling the heat of him even through the hot water, and stroked slowly from base to tip.

Darrokar's head fell back, exposing the long line of his throat. A rumble started deep in his chest, primal and pleased. His hips jerked slightly, pushing into my grip.

"Fuck," he breathed.

I loved that I could do this to him. Reduce the Warrior Lord of Scalvaris to cursing and desperate movements with just my hand. The power of it sang through me, heady and intoxicating.

I stroked him again, learning the feel of him. The ridges along his length that became more pronounced when he was aroused. The way the flexible tip moved independently, seeking and curling. The slickness that his body produced, mixing with the water and making my hand glide smoothly.

His claws dug into my hips, not quite breaking skin but close. A warning or a plea, I couldn't tell which.

"You're trying to kill me," he said, voice strained.

"Just trying to apologize properly." I twisted my wrist on the upstroke, watching his face for his reaction. "Am I doing it right?"

"You're doing it perfectly and you know it."

I grinned and did it again. His tail responded by sliding higher, the tip finding the junction of my thighs and pressing there with seductive intent. I gasped, my rhythm faltering.

"That's cheating," I managed.

"All's fair in apologies and war." His tail moved, stroking through my folds with a precision that made my vision blur. "You started this, luvae. I'm just finishing it."

The tip of his tail found my center and circled, slow and maddening. I tried to keep stroking him, but my coordination was shot, my hand going clumsy as pleasure spiked through me.

He noticed. Of course he noticed. His grin was sharp and satisfied. "Problem?"

"You're impossible."

"You love it."

I did. God help me, I absolutely did.

His tail kept working, alternating between circling my clit and dipping lower to tease my entrance. The dual sensation was overwhelming, made worse by the heat of the water and the steam making it hard to catch my breath. I clung to his shoulders, nails digging in, and let him take me apart.

"Darrokar." His name fell from my lips like a prayer. "Please."

"Please what?" His mouth found my throat, tongue tracing patterns on my skin. "Tell me what you need."

"You. Inside me. Now."

He growled and shifted, his hands lifting me slightly in the water. The tip of his cock pressed against my entrance, hot even through the surrounding heat. Then he pulled me down, filling me in one smooth thrust that made us both groan.

The stretch was intense. Perfect. His length dragged against my inner walls, and that flexible tip immediately started seeking, stroking places that made stars burst behind my eyelids.

I started to move, riding him with a rhythm that had his claws flexing against my hips. His tail was still wrapped around my leg, holding me tight to him. The combination was almost too much, pleasure building faster than I could process.

"That's it," he encouraged, his voice rough. "Take what you need from me."

I used him shamelessly, chasing the building pressure in my core. His hands guided me, helped me find the perfect angle.

When I came, it was with his name on my lips and my body clenching around him hard enough to make him curse. The orgasm rolled through me in waves, each one cresting higher than the last, until I was shaking and boneless in his arms.

He didn't let me rest.

Just shifted his grip, pulling me tighter against his chest, and started moving his hips. Thrusting up into me with a force that would have been too much if the water hadn't cushioned some of the impact.

"My turn," he said against my ear.

His mouth found my breast, tongue circling my nipple before his lips closed around it. He sucked hard, the sensation shooting straight to my core and making me clench around him. His tail resumed its torture, stroking my oversensitive clit with gentle persistence.

I was going to come again. Already. The realization hit me at the same time his flexible tip found that spot inside me that made rational thought impossible.

"Darrokar, I can't. It's too much."

"Yes, you can." His teeth grazed my nipple, just enough pressure to make me gasp. "Give me another one, luvae. Show me you're sorry."

The command in his voice, the absolute certainty that I could do what he demanded, it pushed me over the edge. I came again, harder this time, my body locking up and my vision going white.

Through the haze of my own pleasure, I felt him follow. His hips jerked, his cock pulsing inside me as he filled me with his release. The flexible tip kept moving, kept stroking, drawing out both our pleasure until we were both trembling.

We stayed like that for a long moment, bodies locked together, breathing hard. The water lapped around us, cooling slightly but still warm enough to be comfortable. Steam continued to rise, creating a private world that was just us.

Finally, Darrokar's hands gentled on my hips. His tail unwrapped from my leg, sliding away with one last teasing stroke that made me shiver. He lifted me carefully, letting me slide off him, and settled me back on his lap with my head against his chest.

I could hear his heartbeat, strong and steady beneath my ear.

"Am I forgiven?" I asked quietly.

His chest rumbled with quiet laughter. "You were never really in trouble, luvae. Frustrated, yes. Terrified, absolutely. But not angry."

"Could have fooled me."

"I was angry at the situation. At the warriors who challenged you. At Karyseth for creating an environment where you felt you needed to prove yourself." His hand stroked down my back, claws careful against my skin. "But not at you. Never at you."

The words settled something in my chest that I hadn't realized was unsettled. "I really am sorry I scared you."

"I know." He pressed a kiss to the top of my head. "And I'm proud of you. Even if I wish you'd chosen literally any other way to prove your worth."

"Next year will be different."

His hand stilled on my back. "Next year?"

"I told you. I'm going to win the Skalanth. Just need to train harder, plan better, maybe convince Vega to actually help instead of trying to talk me out of it."

"You're serious."

"Completely." I tilted my head back to look at

him. "You think I'm going to let one loss stop me?"

His expression was complicated. Pride and exasperation and something that might have been resignation. "You're going to be the death of me."

"You've mentioned that." I grinned. "Multiple times, actually."

The water was cooling now, but neither of us moved to get out. This moment felt too good, too peaceful after the chaos of the day. My fingers were starting to prune. But I didn't want to move, didn't want to break this moment of peace and connection.

Eventually, though, practical concerns won out. Darrokar stood, lifting me with him, water streaming off both our bodies. He set me on the edge of the pool and climbed out himself, wings spreading to shake off excess moisture.

I watched him move through the quarters, all lethal grace and controlled power. My mate. My partner. The person who'd tried to stop me today and then supported me anyway when I refused to listen.

He caught me staring and raised an eyebrow. "What?"

"Just appreciating the view."

His mouth curved into a smile that was pure male satisfaction. "The view appreciates being appreciated."

I threw a towel at him. He caught it easily, laughing, and tossed it back. The playfulness felt good after the intensity of the day. Normal. Like we could survive anything as long as we had this.

We dried off and dressed in comfortable clothes. The cuts and bruises from the Skalanth were starting to ache since the adrenaline had fully worn off. I knew I was going to be sore tomorrow. Probably for several days.

Worth it.

Darrokar pulled me back against his chest, wrapping his arms around my waist. His chin rested on top of my head, and I felt the steady rise and fall of his breathing.

"I love you," he said quietly. "Even when you're being reckless and stubborn and making me question every decision that led to us being mated."

"I love you too." I covered his hands with mine, lacing our fingers together. "Even when you're being overprotective and bossy and trying to keep me safe from myself."

"Someone has to."

We stood like that for a while longer, wrapped in each other, looking out the massive window at Scalvaris spread below us. The city glowed, beautiful in its harsh way. The place that had tested me and challenged me and forced me to become stronger than I'd ever thought possible.

This place that was home now, whether I liked it or not.

And I had this. Peace and warmth and the solid presence of my mate at my back.

No one would ever get to take this away from me.

WANT A FREE BONUS STORY?

Sign up at the link below to **receive a free bonus story set in the Drakarn Mates World!**

Get your free bonus story!

https://dl.bookfunnel.com/irp537lyj9

Thank you so much for reading *Daring the Drakarn Warrior Lord*!

Your support means the world to me. If you enjoyed the story, it would mean even more if you could take a moment to share your thoughts in a review or leave a rating.

Hearing from readers like you makes all the difference!

What's next in this series:

Tempted by the Drakarn Shadow

Drakarn Mates

A HARSH DESERT PLANET. Stranded humans. Draconic aliens. A match made in… well, somewhere.

Claimed by the Drakarn Warrior Lord
Echoes of Fire
Scorched by Fate
Fated to the Drakarn Commander
Chained to the Champion
Beast of Ash and Blood
Daring the Drakarn Warrior Lord
Tempted by the Drakarn Shadow

Dragon Brides
Dragon Princes. Fierce Women. Love.
Fated mates, fierce women, and dragon princes
are ready to find their mates.
Also available in audio!

Crux

Ranger

Saber

Cipher

Storm

Drake

Asher

Knox

Flint

Pine

Guarded by the Shifter

Werewolf. Bodyguard. Mate.
The origins of these shifters are shrouded in
mystery, but they're determined to protect their
mates from any harm that comes their way.

Also available in audio!

Hunting Season
On the Prowl
Stalking Magic
Hungry for the Wolf
Wolf Cursed (novella)
Wolf's Temptation

———

Stealing the Alpha

The thief takes what she wants, but the alpha keeps what's his...

Join shifter thief Mel as she clashes with lion alpha Luke in an explosive trilogy of two opposites who can't keep away from one another.

Also available in audio!

The Alpha Heist
Entangled with the Thief
In the Alpha's Bed

———

Alien Mates: Planet Exile

Guerran is no place for pretty human women. But these alien heroes will protect their mates!

Also available in audio!

Exile's Hunter

Exile's Adored

Zulir Warrior Mates

Kidnapped humans. Alien Warriors. Electric wings.

The Zulir Warrior Mates series brings you human heroines and heroes abducted from Earth who find love – and wings! – with the alien warriors who rescue them.

Also available in audio!

Synnr's Saint

Synnr's Hope

Synnr's Spark

Synnr's Kiss

Synnr's Ride

Mated to the Alien

Fated Mate Alien Romance

Detyens are doomed to die young if they don't find their fated mates.

Follow along as these mated pairs fight off aliens, corrupt dictators, prejudiced humans, pirates, and more! The books can be read or listened to in any order, though some characters show up in multiple stories.

Select books available in audio.

Pick a book and jump into the action today!

Ruwen

Tyral

Stoan

Cyborg

Krayter

Kayleb

Shayn

Braxtyn

Doryan

Dekon

Detyen Warriors

Detya was destroyed a hundred years ago. These doomed warriors are out to find justice… and their mates.

The Detyen Warriors series brings you kick butt heroines, alpha alien heroes, fated mates, and relationships strong enough to span the galaxy!

The entire series is also available in audio!

Soulless

Ruthless

Heartless

Faultless

Endless

———

Detyen Warrior Outcasts
Fated Mate Alien Romance

These doomed warriors were abandoned by their people and live on the edge. Their mates hold the key to their salvation.

Pick a book and jump into the action today!

Also available in audio!

Dangerous Bond

Intrepid Bond

Wayward Bond

Alien Holiday Romance

Christmas… in space????
These alien holiday romances look beyond Earth's winter holidays and ring in the season across the galaxy!
Select titles available in audio.
Snowed in with the Alien Beast
The Alien's Winter Gift
The Alien Reindeer's Wild Ride
Trapped with her Alien Mate

Alien Outlaws

Outlaws, schemes, and love… it's all there in the Alien Outlaws series…
Andie Munster is sick of life on Ixilta, the planet she got dumped on after being abducted from Earth six years ago. And when the mysterious and dangerous Xandr shows up looking for a way off the planet, she's half-prisoner, half-co-conspirator in a wild rush to escape.

Also available in audio!

Rogue Alien's Escape

Rogue Alien's Woman

Rogue Alien's Secret

Rogue Alien's Legacy

———

Find more by Kate Rudolph at www.

katerudolph.net

ABOUT KATE RUDOLPH

KATE RUDOLPH IS a paranormal and sci-fi romance writer who lives in Indiana. She loves writing about kick butt heroines and the steamy heroes who love them. She's been devouring romance novels since she was too young to be reading them and had to hide her books so no one would take them away. She couldn't imagine a better job in this world than writing romances and sharing them with her fellow readers.

If you enjoyed this story, please consider leaving a review.